Dedicated to
the people and streets of Melbourne
and Paul

CONTENTS

Dear Stranger 6

Chapter 1. Strange Beginnings 10

Chapter 2. Her Garden 28

Chapter 3. Three Eyes 42

Chapter 4. Ghost of Gonzo 56

Chapter 5. Concrete Forest 82

Chapter 6. It's About Time 114

Photographs 130

About the Authors 136

Dear Stranger,

The city killed me. The street saved me. It set fire to my soul.
It burned the sight into me. So I could see. All those invisible
stories, hiding in the deep, dark depths of the street's fragmented
reality.

Everyday. At 11:11. I would visit the NGV. To watch the bathing
man: a middle-aged man with orange hair, frazzled from his
scalp as if lightning had struck. He was always there, under cloud
and sun, no matter the weather. Diving deep into the depths of
the fountain. Collecting silver wishes in the form of cold change.
Everyday. Until COVID passed away.

The man dived, always, in the same green trousers and
soggy shoes he trailed through the city. His daily path, marked by
size-10 puddles. One day, when the sun stopped shining, I asked
him why he dived.

He told me, coughing from the cold, 'I dive because I
refuse to beg.'

He dived because a part of him was already dead. He dived
because COVID made strangers sick, and their wishes for health
were thrown into the fountain. Which he collected, and used, to
feed.

He liked to call himself: *the dream eater.*

Everyday. From two to four. Outside the State Library. I would
watch the hanging-jawed mute wander the gardens. Limping
from stranger to stranger, dribbling, carrying a bin-bag of hand-

written stories everywhere he went. And a cardboard sign gripped between his track-marked hands: *I'm a mute. Any spare change?*

Every now and then, a stranger would dig through their pockets, flick a coin his way, and feel somewhat better about their day. But what the strangers didn't know was that I had heard the mute talk, icy, fast and erratic, to his friends on the street. But only when nobody else was watching. And the stories he shared from the depths of his bin-bag were all purposefully written like a six-year-old. Strangely twisted. To squeeze another dollar from the same stranger he'd just fooled. His mute-mouth was all an act.

Everyday at five, I would talk to John on the corner of Bourke Street. An old man with thick hands and a bushy beard, sitting on a green milk crate cushioned by cardboard. He liked to call it 'the seat of the street.'

He liked to show me his teeth. White, clean, a holy sort of pristine. Ten years ago, a young lady gave him a toothbrush. The brush was brown and wiry, and he always said to me, 'This is my lucky toothbrush. I've had it for ten years. Somebody special gave it to me. She told me it's blessed. I believe her. Look at my teeth. They haven't aged a day since I received the brush. Make sure you brush your teeth! Your smile is the only thing you can control in this world. Everything else is up to god-awful fate.'

I arrived in this city when the world was locked-down. When strangers refused to look at me, talk to me, accept me for who I am. A foreigner. So I spent everyday, from sunrise to sunset, wandering alone from street to street as a stranger from another place. Watching the pantomime playing on the cold-hard concrete stage of the city. Writing, recording, scribbling every time I met someone new. Every character, every story, every act. They all found a home in my little black notebook.

But where was my home?

I wish I could find someone else like me, someone who carries their own little black notebook full of strange stories, hoping to find meaning in the madness.

Could it be you?

Are you out there somewhere?

If you are, please contact me.

There's a tale to this city

STRANGE BEGINNINGS

RICK WALKOW

'So ... you just left?'

'I've been there for too long,' I said, gazing into the foggy window. Lauren took away the empty coffee cup from my table. I'd met her a year ago, when I first became a regular at the cafe. Back then I used to order the same cup of English Breakfast tea every day, until one time she stopped me at the counter.

'Oh, can't you just change it up a bit?'

'No.'

She tilted her head. *'No?'* Against my will, she made me a long black. Since then, I'd ordered a long black every day and Lauren became a friend.

'So now what?' she asked me.

I had just left my job as a bookseller and needed to spend some time alone. I didn't have anywhere to go. Home was a hotel without a neon sign and I was getting sick of the old folks chasing their kids down in the suburbs. The coffee shop near the train station was the only place where I could find a sliver of peace. I planned to spend most of my time reading pieces from magazines or writing short stories to keep myself afloat.

I looked up at her. 'I'm just writing,' I said, 'so I don't run out of money.'

Lauren nodded, uninterested. She went back to the counter.

My eyes returned to my computer screen. I saw an email from some guy named Jay. The email didn't have any formatting

11

to it, like jumbled word-vomit. I furrowed my brows and read the first line:

Fan of your work, are you free later on this week? I would love to show you some hidden parts of the city.

'What's tripping you up now?' Lauren was back at my table because the place was quiet and she was clearly bored.

I pointed at my screen. 'There's someone named Jay who wants to meet me.'

'Sounds sketchy,' she said. 'What for?'

'By the looks of it, he's another writer,' I said, scrolling down a little more.

Lauren shook her head, smirking. 'One of you is enough.' She left my table. I chuckled and continued reading the email.

Flinders Street station, at 10 am.

It was Monday and the weather was warm. I slung my satchel over my shoulder and stepped into the train carriage. A golf course whizzed past and I thought about the guy from the email. I couldn't figure him out. I thought that coffee would be the gateway to getting to know Jay, who was proficient in word-vomiting via email.

The train pulled into the station. We were scheduled to meet at ten, but after an agonising fifteen-minute wait, the word-vomitter tottered up to me in flip-flops and a t-shirt with three half-naked ladies printed on it.

'Hey mate!' he shouted. 'I'm sorry.'

I looked at him from head to toe and thought, *okay then.*

I had assumed he was also from Melbourne. Maybe more seasoned in this city than me. But I was wrong.

JAY KHAN

I saw Rick standing alone outside Flinders Street station, sweating, pacing, itching his head. I yelled from a distance, cutting my way through a sea of strangers, making sure nobody stepped on my feet.

'I missed the tram, so I ran here.' I panted, removing my right flip-flop, pushing the plastic Y back into the socket. 'Good as new.'

Wide-eyed, Rick glared at the breasts printed on my t-shirt. Dabbing sweat from his forehead with a red-and-white checkered cloth.

'What the hell is that?' I jerked back, pointing at his handkerchief.

'What?'

'That!'

Rick flailed the handkerchief across his face, folded it into a perfect square and slipped it inside his shirt pocket.

'Anyways, I hope you get to meet the mute today ... he's not actually a mute, but that's his act on the street to make some money,' I rambled without context. 'Ahh ... and the bathing man has been pretty active recently. At some point, let's pop down to the NGV fountain to have a look.' I paused, expecting an excited answer from Rick. But he said nothing. Instead his eyes hovered over my bare toes.

I itched my chin. 'So ... do you want to take me to a cafe, or shall I take you?'

Rick fixed his collar, shrugged his shoulders. 'I'll take you! I'm from here. I know a good place.'

En route to the cafe, I pointed out various locations along the way, retelling the stories I'd collected from them. 'You see that church staircase over there?' I shouted through the hum of passing trams, pointing at a stone staircase leading to God's big red door. 'That was where I used to talk to the lady with three eyes. Two made by God, the other tattooed (I stuck my finger into the creases of my forehead) right here! How about that?'

Rick trailed ahead, umming and ahhing with distant eyes, as if his body belonged to the moment but his spirit was already far, far away in some distant cafe. Our feet stuttered through the streets, passing occupied milk crates on every corner. 'You got any change? Any spare change?' strangers whimpered from their crates, rubbing their fingers together as if they were trying to conjure up some sort of economico electro-magnetism.

'Turn here,' Rick said.

Before pulling around the concrete corner, I bumped Rick on the shoulder. 'What do milk crates make you think of?'

Rick fumbled around in his pocket. 'I don't know. Milk in bottles, I guess? Hang on ... I need to find my pen. I'm sure it was in my bag.'

'Right,' I replied.

Knowing the stories weren't helping his mood.

RICK WALKOW

'So, what's your story?'

We sat outside under an umbrella, even though it wasn't raining. The sun peaked its head and I flinched at the couple next to our table, drinking hot coffee on a hot day. Jay didn't answer my question. He just laughed and off he went, talking in the same way as that jumbled email. The only word that I caught onto was *street*.

I lifted my coffee cup and took a sip. 'I mean ...' I said, 'why are we here?'

'Well, I want to show you a different part of the city.'

I chuckled. 'I don't know about that. I think I've seen most of it.'

As a Melburnian for most of my life, I'd had a lot of time to explore the city. I had always loved wandering around alone. Dad said I'd stay that way—alone—if I kept that abrasive temper of mine.

Jay had a smile on his face like he was high on the summer's air. 'Yeah?'

'I'm not sure I know what we're trying to do here.'

The same smile. 'Yeah? Do you have something in mind?' He stood from his chair and walked into the cafe to pay.

I followed him to the entrance of the cafe. 'Stopping by Dymocks doesn't sound bad,' I said. He didn't hear me. After paying, he stepped out and nudged me.

'Just follow. You'll get the hang of it.'

'The hang of what?'

I traced his steps down a few alleyways. Dymocks bookstore was across the street and I pointed at the entrance.

Jay shook his head. 'Yeah? Shut the books for once today.'

'But ... aren't we writers?'

'This is different.'

He dragged me into a side alley. The brick walls on either side were covered in street art, picture frames, and broken glass.

I halted my steps. 'Jay.'

'Yeah?' The smile this time had a hint of victory in it.

'Where the hell are you taking me?'

He smirked. 'The Land of Sunshine. I thought you knew this city.'

'Of course I do.'

'Not this part, obviously. Like I said ... different parts of the city.'

'This is ...' I stood in the middle of the lane and stared at a piece of jagged glass sticking out of the wall. 'This place is new, right?'

'No.' He leaned a little deeper into the shade. 'It was already here when I arrived a few months back.'

'You're not from Melbourne?' I stepped back, waiting for him to spit out his words.

'No, why would I be?' he giggled. 'I'm from the UK.'

Just before I could conjure up a response, Jay tapped my shoulder and turned me round. 'Look ...'

A squeaky sound passed by.

JAY KHAN

RITTLE! RATTLE! SWOOOOOOSH! When we turned the corner, an elderly Asian couple, both dressed in pink, swooshed past us, nearly hitting our hips with their empty shopping trolley. Rick sprung back. RITTLE! RATTLE! the wheels went against the concrete. 'Hurry up! Hurry up!' they yelled in Mandarin at each other. 'We're going to be late!' Until their words droned into the distance.

'What the hell?' Rick grumbled.

SNIP! SNAP! A man sitting on a blue milk crate under a rig of scaffolding, wearing a bin-bag around his neck, snipped and snapped at clumped black hair with a pair of garden shears.

'Hey! You!' a croaky voice from the end of the alleyway yelled. 'Say cheese!'

Our eyes traced the voice to a strange bulge of purple fluff, sticking out from behind a green recycling bin. The bin rattled, thudded, and then OOMMPPHHH! The voice behind the bin kicked it out of the way, revealing a little bald lady wearing a purple dressing gown, sitting on a piece of cardboard. SNAP! SNAP! SNAP! her shrivelled fingers went against the trigger of a yellow disposable camera. 'Gotcha!'

A half-lit cigarette burned between her lips. 'Come here and get a picture! Don't be shy sweet fellas!' Her head bobbled left, right, up, down, shaking, as if a cattle prod was jammed into the back of her neck. Her cigarette held onto her gums like a bucking bronco, flicking ash in every direction.

SNAP! SNAP! SNAP! her camera went.

'Hehe! Come here, so I can get a good look at both of you!'

SNIP! SNAP! The man with garden shears stared at Rick with old, worn-out eyes. Dark circles ran around his gaze.

The lady clicking her camera croaked, 'Come on! I don't bite!'

Rick looked at me with dilated pupils, sweat dripping from his bushy black hair in thick beads. 'Jay ... What is this place? Why did you take me here?'

'Are you coming or what?' yelled the lady.

SNAP! SNAP! the camera went.

SNIP! SNAP! the shears went.

Rick went to say something, but I slapped him on the back. 'Stop your jibba-jabba. Come on.' Drenched in sweat, Rick slid a pair of slippery fingers into his black over-the-shoulder satchel, pulling out a pocket-sized leather notebook and a delicate fountain pen.

'You coming or what?' I asked. 'No good writing from your imagination. Come and hear the story yourself if you want to write it!'

Rick snarled with static feet, throwing his mind into the pages of his notebook. Pretending to scribble. The man with garden shears kept him in his dead-fish gaze, snip-snapping in the shadows.

When I reached the lady, she asked, 'What's wrong with your friend?' with a gummy smile while fiddling with her saggy breasts. 'Is he ladyshy?'

'Oi! You!' She winked at Rick. 'You scared to talk to a real lady? Huh!'

Rick backed away.

'He ain't scared of old Jim over there with his big bloody scissors. Why's he afraid of me?' Before I had the chance to reply, she snapped, 'Do you wanna hear a joke or what!'

'Sure.'

She dropped her camera to the floor, pulled the cigarette out and twitched it between her bony fingers. 'Why can't I take a good picture these days?'

I asked her, 'Why?'

'Because you can't get a fella to stand still long enough to get 'em in foc—'

I noticed Rick in great distress, wiping bead after bead of sweat with his red-and-white handkerchief, turning his head every other second towards the man and his dead-fish stare.

THEN! he stormed off without a word. Clenching his notebook tightly between his red hands.

'Chat another time,' I said to the lady.

'But ... wait! You didn't hear the joke.'

I dashed after Rick.

RICK WALKOW

I watched the streets with widened eyes. Jay came up to me and
whacked me on the shoulder. 'You feeling alright?'

'I … ehh …' I looked down at my notebook.

He took it off me and pressed the notebook against his face.
'I can't read any of this!' he mumbled. 'You were ladyshy back
there, weren't you?'

'I'm a hack.' I snatched my notebook back and shoved it into
my satchel.

Jay's shirt was halfway drenched in sweat. The sun was no
longer lingering near the edges of the clouds. The glare from the
concrete path hurt my eyes.

'Say …' I looked at Jay. 'Where can we get a drink around
here?'

The same amused smile. 'I thought you knew the city better
than me?'

'Give me a break. Where?'

Jay took me to a little Italian place. We sat on the stools at
the counter. It was boiling inside and the smell of Italian food made
me feel sick. Jay scanned the bar and whispered, 'Did you know
the previous owner got stabbed?'

The Italian barman came over and gave us a smile. 'How can
I help you today?'

Jay ordered two granitas. The barman nodded and reached a spoon into a cooler and poured us two glasses. It was a fine iced watermelon drink. I downed the first glass and the smell of food no longer disgusted me. Jay's eyes wandered around the espresso bar. They went from the coffee machine, to the cooler, and then landed on my ass.

'What the hell are you staring at?'

'Do you want to hear a strange story about the seat you're sitting in?'

JAY KHAN

DIRTY ESPRESSO

'I saw a man sitting alone, where you're sitting right now. He was writing with a fountain pen made of solid gold. He had a brown leather notebook, full to the brim with multi-coloured sticky notes. The stubble on his face, the squint of his eyes, the way he wrote. It all told a story whether he knew it or not. I just knew, by looking at him, he had truly lived.'

Rick took a gulp from his granita. Strangers floated in and out of the bar, mumbling loudly, proudly. A moustachio fat lady with a twitching left eye slurped on her cappuccino behind us. SLURP! SLURP! SLURP! She slurped like she wanted a chat. Steam from the coffee machine boiled in our ears. Knives and forks rattled in the dishwasher. Rocco the barman hummed old-school Italian songs to himself patiently, merrily, as if he was living in a dream.

But the story I told was not as merry as the soothing songs.

'I asked the man what he was writing and he said nothing special,' I told Rick. 'Then we talked about everything. The weather. COVID. Life. He told me he'd lived in Tokyo for ten years as a manager of a five-star resort owned by the Yakuza.'

'The what?' Rick interrupted.

'You've never heard of the Japanese mafia?'

'Huh?'

'Never mind. As I was saying: the man's voice was soft, his eyes blue, but his face looked hardened. He didn't want to tell me his age, but I believe he was over fifty ...'

Rocco the barman came over, smiling at our empty glasses. 'You guys want some more?'

'I'm okay, thank you,' I said.

Rick turned to me. 'Go on.'

Strangers continued to pass in and out of the bar. The moustachio lady stopped her slurps and became still as a statue, latching onto my every word.

So, I asked the man what he was doing with his time nowadays. He said that he was taking it easy. Had a few properties here and there and didn't need to work. Then he took his espresso shot, yelled for another and continued: "Now I spend most of my time in cafes, just writing down feelings, reflecting on the shit I did in the past. People often assume I'm some fancy writer when they see my pen. But I'm no writer, trust me. I'm just some fella with too much time on his hands and a fancy pen. That's all. The Japanese gave me this pen as my leaving present. 24 carat gold. It's a bloody beaut. I take it everywhere I go."

The man then asked me what my story was and why I was there … "This is a Tuesday afternoon. You got nothing better to do?"

I told him, "I got two weeks off work. A steel pole fell on my head. Cracked it open like an egg. I didn't want to mope around at home so I thought I should get out of the house and talk to some people, smell the air."

"Good on ya! Did you talk to many people today?"

"Sure … a few. You, and some people I know living on the street."

"What?" the man said. Something changed in his face. "How d'ya know them?"

"I'm sorry, who?"

The man pulled his stool closer to me, staring into my eyes with bloodshot pupils. His fingers tapped erratically on the wooden counter. "You heard what I said, kid. How d'ya know them?"

"Who's them?" I asked.

"The hobos."

"I don't know. I just talk to them."

"You shouldn't do that!" he yelled. The rest of the bar looked at us.

"Why not?"

"Because. Because they're dangerous. I tell ya! Stay away from them. Didn't your parents teach you? Stranger danger, ya fucking dumb cunt."

"I'm not a kid. I'm twenty-four."

"I don't give a shit how old you are. Ya gotta be careful, kid. There's monsters out there. Monsters you won't believe. I've seen them with my own eyes!" His eyelids fluttered. His pupils vibrated. His fingers tapped against his thigh over twisted silence. "Listen to me!" The silence broke as he grabbed my right arm tight, leaning into my face. "I know a woman who happily killed a man! Ya know? Killed! Without feeling an inch of guilt! She can't. Even if she tried. She was so hurt as a little girl, now she can't feel a thing. And you're talking to strangers when her kind are out there?" His nails sunk into my wrist. "Ya feel it? She couldn't! She could slit your throat without a flinch. Hell, she might even get off on it. She was abused in ways you can't even imagine. Do you know what that does to your soul? Do ya? Do you really?"

I looked at him with blank eyes.

"Do ... do ya?' His voice trembled. Tears rolled down his cheeks. His hand gripping me shivered. "Do ya?!"

I winced at the pain from his nail marks. "No ... I don't."

"Last month she met a man. A young fella, not much younger than you, down at Flinders. They got along. So, she invited him back to her place to show him the ropes. The man thought, why not? He wanted a fuck, but he was fucked proper. When they got to her place, she tied the rope around his neck til his face turned blue like a bloody blueberry. He was only a young fella. No one knew about it. She laughed when she told me the story."

"She never got caught, ya know? I saw her last week at the pub drinking a gin. They never found the kid's body. She joked and told me she chopped him up into little pieces and ate him over a week ..." The trembling eased a little. "I feel sorry ... For the lady. Not the man. The man didn't feel her pain. It was fast for

24

him. But the lady, she died fifty times over. You could see it in her
eyes. Nothing there. Just empty holes where her soul used to be. It
wasn't the lady who killed the man. It was her father and his dirty
cock."

I ended the story. Gulped the granita. Looked Rick in the eyes and
said, 'Strange story, eh?'

Rick said nothing. He looked around, left to right, squeezing
the stool he was sitting on. He clenched his fingers, scratched his
ear, and looked worried as if the man with the golden pen could
arrive at any moment.

The mustachio lady left without a word. Rocco the barman
merrily sung his song, as if all I'd told was just another story at the
espresso bar.

RICK WALKOW

By the time we walked out of the bar, it was already dark. The
flickering neon sign outside the espresso bar painted the alleyway
red. From the entrance, I could still hear the barman's hum. It was
a good folk song but something about that story tinted it and turned
it into a haunted lullaby, at a bar with a twisted tale.

'Come on.' Jay tapped me on the shoulder. 'It's getting late.'
I walked over to the station in a daze.

I returned to the cafe the next morning and opened my notebook at my usual table. I was trying to make sense of what happened yesterday.

'What the hell is that?' Lauren leaned over, holding my coffee, and looked into my notebook. She saw my scribbles: *The Land of Sunshine.*

'A gift from Jay.'

'That writer you met?'

'Yeah, him.'

It was seven in the morning and the sun was lurking behind the clouds again. The cafe was cool. More and more yuppies populated the train station outside.

'Still sounds sketchy to me,' she said, placing my coffee on the table. 'This Jay business sounds whack. Here's your usual.'

I closed my notebook. 'I don't know …' An announcement boomed outside and the train station cleared. I smiled. 'I quite like him.'

There's a tale to this city

HER GARDEN

JOHNNY LOCK

The night before I was supposed to meet Jay for the first time, I decided to bail. He would just find me intolerable anyway. I'm too paranoid for people like him. Outgoing. Confident. All the things that I am not. I've locked myself away for so long that I've forgotten who I am.

Jay had taken an interest in my work. Typewritten poems stuck up around the city for strangers to read. And I'd taken an interest in his work. Handwritten letters stuck up around the city, for the same strangers to read. In a way, we were in the same line of work, which wasn't even really work at all. It was only natural we'd meet up at some point. But when it came to it, my body seized up from the hammering in my chest. You'd think someone had tried to mug me in my own bedroom, the way I was out of breath.

I told Jay I wouldn't be meeting him and crawled up to sleep.

In the morning, I changed my mind. I told Jay to meet me at Flinders in an hour. My heart was no longer racing. I gathered all the poems I'd typed up a few nights before and slipped them into the cover of my black notebook. I slipped my pen in the breast pocket of my navy-blue jacket and my pack of cigarettes in my jeans. Zipped up my bag and slung it over my shoulder. The bookcase behind me beckoned me not to leave. There were stories there already, so why did I need to go off and find my own with this stranger?

In the kitchen, my mother had the same enthusiasm as my bookcase. Sometimes she forgot how old I was. Her smothering was wearing thin and she was yet to catch on, even as my facial hair started to grow in and I'd worked out how to manage my money without her help.

'You've never met this man before?' she asked me.

I stared her dead between the eyes. 'No.'

'So, you're meeting up with a stranger.'

'Everyone's a stranger at first, Ma. Until they're not.'

She winced as if I'd told her that her cooking was too salty, or the smell of her cigarette smoke was trailing through the house, which it always was. 'The city is dangerous. You see the news. Every day someone gets followed or king-hit or killed. Remember Bourke Street? Drivers around there are crazy. And the junkies everywhere. I hate the city for that reason.'

'Ma.'

'Why do you have to go to the city? Someone like you, you're an easy target.'

'Ma!'

Her body slackened and she turned away from me. 'Bloody hell. Just be careful. Text me when you're there, please. Don't get the train too late. The train is full of junkies at night.'

I grunted and left the kitchen. I'd locked myself away for so long, dreaming without actually doing, simply because my mother had fed me the idea—that slim possibility—that if I ventured too far from home, I would end up as another victim on TV. No wonder I was so paranoid all the time. The city made me nervous. But I was by no means terrified to walk down its streets or stay out late. Not like her.

I got off the train and headed to the station steps to meet Jay. I wouldn't be doing street poetry at all, had I never encountered Jay's letters to strangers during lockdown. Had I not seen his devilish smile all over the internet. Had I not heard of his interactions with the streets of Melbourne. The city I called home, without actually exploring. How could it ever be home, if I didn't even know where Swanston Street was?

Jay's tall, lanky frame came into view and the nerves fell away, as if I was meeting up with an old friend instead of a new one. He walked with an energetic bounce. His eyes were a grey-blue radiating the same madness of the streets that he claimed to be so familiar with.

'I've just come back from confession,' he said.

I blinked. 'Confession?'

'Yeah.'

He dropped the conversation there, as if he wanted to say something I might not have wanted to hear, retreating into himself. His eyes went blank as we crossed the road. I could see he was in need of a caffeine hit. I was too.

JAY KHAN

My thoughts ran back an hour, to the priest's words: 'I can't call the exorcist unless you bring your friend to me, so I can see the marks.'

The night before, my friend had showed me his scars. Three-finger claw marks made by a demon. They were getting more and more frequent. My friend was starting to worry. Ever since he was a kid, his skin would burn at random. On the tram. At work. In bed. And when he rolled his sleeves up to look at the burns, he always found the same three-finger claw marks. When I asked about the demon, he told me about his childhood addiction to the occult. How he played ouija boards the way a kid plays Crash Bandicoot. I couldn't stop thinking about the marks.

Three fingers.

Three claws.

It reminded me of Bob.

JOHNNY LOCK

We waited for our orders outside a cafe in a dingy alley, where I had posted one of my poems. It was still there. Jay handed me my coffee with a cautious expression, distant and far away even though he was right beside me. I was feeling slow, but I imagined he'd slipped something into my coffee, because the first few sips turned me into a burning firecracker on the lookout for sparks on the street. The ashes of monotony. I felt myself falling back into my nonsensical rambles, disguised as poetry. He filmed me sticking up a poem. I could feel the brand of his phone camera on the back of my head.

Jay shot a blue-eyed glower across the road and turned to me. 'Johnny. Stay here, mate. I'll be back in a minute. Just stay here, okay?'

He wandered off to speak to a man with one arm, murmuring to himself where he squatted. My conditioned instinct to flee from danger prickled up at his warning. *Stay back? What the fuck did that mean? Is he putting himself in danger? Shit. Is he putting me in danger?*

JAY KHAN

I saw him. Sitting alone, muttering to himself, biting on a dollar coin, trying to bend it out of shape with his six remaining teeth. I looked. He saw my eyes, and I asked him, 'Hey mate, do you want me to get you a cappuccino from over the road?'

'FUCK OFF YA COW CUNT!' He spat the coin from his mouth, got up, fiddled with the stump where his arm used to be, and pressed his face against mine during a global pandemic, screaming, 'I fucking told you to fuck off yesterday. I wanted a black coffee, and what does this cunt give me? A fucking coffee that tastes like a cow. Gahhhh! Next time, just give me money, will ya?'

He scratched the welts and track marks running down his neck. 'If you get me a cow coffee again, I will pull my fucking eyes out and throw them at you. Gahhhhh!'

Johnny watched the interaction from behind, as if he'd just stepped into a movie he never bought the ticket for. The eyes, the grimace, the fidgeting fingers, his face told it all. That same face of worry I'd seen countless times before, on the others I took out to the street, before they left without saying goodbye.

But instead of walking away, Johnny looked at me, silent for a moment, before asking, 'What was all that about?'

'Ah, nothing really. I bought that guy a coffee yesterday and apparently today he doesn't like milk. He's cooked up on something rotten, because he wasn't like this yesterday. Sometimes you just can't help those who hate to be helped.'

'You tried your best.' Johnny smiled. One of those smiles that indicated he understood ... but he probably didn't. And instead of leaving like they normally did, he started talking about everything and nothing without a filter or a place to stop. Rambling past his point again and again, twisting it into another point he hadn't thought about. I liked that about him. When he rambled and rambled and rambled, his eyes shone like jades in the sky, green on the verge of blue, a bit like mine. Half-mad when he wanted to be.

JOHNNY LOCK

On Bourke Street, I looked at Jay and pointed at a lady sitting on cold concrete with her trolley full of plastic yellow flowers beside her. She had an interesting clothing style—a padded pink jumper, a pink hat, even pink socks.

'I wonder what that lady's story is,' I said.

'Well. You're about to find out. Let's go talk to her.'

We strode up to the woman and my mind already had the beginnings of a poem going.

The lady in pink.

JAY KHAN

Julie looked embarrassed by her age. She carried around a little
garden made of plastic flowers and broken dreams. Large heavy-
duty earmuffs hung around her neck. Her eyes were clear and soft.
Her jacket was clean and pink.

'Police scare me,' she said, shifting and swinging her eyes.
A police van crawled past without a siren. She dug her fingers into
her ears and squinted. 'Ahhhhhhhh!'

Johnny and I exchanged glances.

'The sirens are so loud. They're for me, they're coming for
me.' After the silent van left, she pointed at a pair of pink handcuffs
hanging from her little garden. 'I hate them. They're watching
me. Always! They know I know. You see this!' She pointed at her
wrist. 'You see this scar? The police tied their handcuffs around
my wrist, so tight, I can no longer feel three of my fingers. See!
Look!' I looked and found no scar. 'I can't move them!' she cried,
shaking her fingers. 'They cut the nerves completely. People like
us, you know, you and me, we get trampled on so often because of
THEM.'

The street sweeper swept past, swerving between oncoming
strangers.

'Ahhhhhh!' she yelled. 'You see that?' Pointing at the
sweeper. Her energy trembled. Her torment fractured her
sentences. Her lips quivered. 'You see the way he looked at me?
He's always after me, I can see it in his eyes.' I frowned, feeling

the goosebumps running up the back of my neck. 'He's got the look, like them. The ones who are out to outbreed the whiteness from people like you and me.'

I blinked.

It hit me like a bitter lemon.

The connection was cut.

'Look at the colour of his skin!' she hissed. "Just look at it! There's too many Asians in Melbourne. Too many foreigners. They're taking over our country. Times have changed. Us white folk are now a minority. It's sickening. What happened to the good ol' days?'

I think I knew why the lady lived on the street.

Maybe.

Just maybe.

Times needed to change and she'd refused to accept it. Resisting, resisting, resisting, in a world that only made sense to her. Full of self-pity on the street.

JOHNNY LOCK

Julie in pink, Julie and her handcuffs, Julie with her fingers in her ears.

Paranoia steamed off her white, weathered skin from years of living on the street. She showed us her wrist and told us about the police handcuffs that had left permanent scars, but we didn't see any. Just a bony wrist and jittery eyes when we met her gaze, which she never held for long because she hated eye contact. If it was a mental scar she was referring to, I knew all about those. I was full of them. Why else would I turn to the street for poetry? It became my meditation and without it I would never have met Jay. He drew the madness out of me, the way a syringe drew the blood before that hit of poisonous bliss.

I'd been watching Trainspotting too much.

Listening to Julie, I was struck with a peculiar sense that there was some ironic purpose in my being there, in my crossing paths with this woman. It was as if she was a reflection of myself—the paranoia, the hatred and fear for everything outside of herself—and that she'd been presented to me as a challenge to my own unshakable flaw. Julie was the physical embodiment of the choice I had to make: be paranoid forever and live in misery, or learn to overcome it and embrace myself.

When we headed back to Jay's apartment, it dawned on me that I'd never actually been into a skyrise apartment before, or any kind of apartment. How closed off had my upbringing been? I might as well have walked the streets with him wearing a bib and chewing on a dummy. I did suck on a dummy until I was six, after all. What was another sixteen years?

I met his girlfriend Echo. No doubt she bore witness to the unshakeable introversion that poured out of me like sweat, which I carried around the way Julie carries her trolley and her invisible scars.

Jay showed me some of his books he kept locked away. The ones he lugged around with him after all that travelling. He was a collector of stories, a walking embodiment of truth and raw grit, a straight-to-the-point, no beat-around-the-bush sort of guy.

'How about we write our pieces about the strangers we met today?' he asked.

What he meant was— *we're writing those damned pieces, let's go.*

We sat down and gathered our thoughts, triggering our memories and takeaways from every moment on the street that day. Jay wrote a letter in his classic style with the smiley face at the end. It was surreal watching him work, like I wasn't just interacting with him through a screen. I was part of the story. I was there.

I wrote my poem about Julie and was immediately filled with insecurity. But Jay seemed to like it, so I started to like it too.

'Thanks, man. I just depend on validation too much.'

'Shut up. Just shut up. Let's just finish these pieces and post them around. Okay?'

'Let's do it.'

I waved goodbye to Echo. Behind her I saw my reflection in the balcony window and waved at that too. Goodbye to the scared me, the one I was choosing to leave behind. It wasn't going to be as easy as that, though.

JULIE

Julie in pink
   Julie in a hat
      Julie with her mask on chin;
Julie embarrassed by her age
   Julie of the people and the world
      Julie and her pull-along trolley;
Julie and her handcuffs
   Julie and her fingers in her ears
      Julie and her earmuffs;
Julie hates police sirens
   Julie fears street cleaners
      Julie lives in a long-gone past;
Julie sounds like she could cry
   Julie is filled with cynicism
      Julie hides this from me;
Julie lives a dual life
   Julie is lying to me
      Julie doesn't know i see;
Julie cowers at noises
   Julie waits before she speaks
      Julie speaks before she thinks;
Julie tells me all i need to know
   Julie hasn't wasted my time
      Julie has taught me plenty.

JAY KHAN

Night had eaten the sun. Stars replaced the clouds. The streets were emptying. While posting our letters and poems on the corner of Swanston Street, Johnny got a call. His posture changed, his neck arched, his voice went shy and quiet, as if he didn't want me to hear.

'Yeah, Ma?' he whispered.

I could hear his brain moving in circles, his eyes wandering here, there, everywhere, wide and sorry, as if to say this wasn't him. He rushed to a corner and started talking fast and erratic, like the strangers on the street.

'Don't worry, I'm fine,' he whispered, cupping his mouth with his hands. 'Nothing happened, Ma. He's safe. He's not bloody dangerous.'

He pulled away from the phone, flustered and hunched.

I asked him, 'You all good, mate?'

Johnny snapped, 'I'm fine. Why?'

'Nothing.'

'I've got to head off now, Jay. But I'll see you again soon.'

Before I could say bye, another call came in. He put it off until he was far enough from me that I wouldn't hear.

THREE EYES

RICK WALKOW

The early morning's weather was mild, but the heat was closing in. I drained my coffee, looked into the cup, empty, like the cafe. I stood up from my seat and headed for the door.

'Off so soon?' Lauren said.

I halted my steps, looked at my watch. It was nine. 'Yeah, off to a meet-up with a poet and that Jay guy.'

'Oh … him again …' She wiped the bench and chucked the towel in the sink. 'And a poet? How'd you meet?'

'I met him through a photo I took,' I said, turning towards the counter and pulling up a picture of Flinders Street station on my phone. 'I took this one and, here …' I pointed at a guy smoking a cigarette in the foreground. 'This is the poet.'

'But … have you actually met him?' She squinted. 'It's just a photo.'

'I posted it and a day later I got a message from this guy. He said he's friends with Jay. Today we're all going to meet up.'

'So …' Lauren looked at the edgy figure with the cigarette and curly hair. 'You've never met this guy before … are you going to be okay?'

I shrugged, said goodbye, and stepped onto the early train.

I leaned against the window and listened to the carriage's hum. When it stopped at a station, an empty coffee cup rolled by my foot and I thought about Jay. He knew my city better than I did. In Melbourne, 'getting coffee' had a very specific connotation. It was a kind of art here. But for Jay, his art was the courage that brought him down into the gritty parts of the city. And coffee, for him, was the gateway drug to the stories of the streets.

JOHNNY LOCK

I'd first heard of Rick Walkow a few months earlier. He lived his life like a proper writer. I saw him once, at Flinders Street, by total chance, but didn't have the energy or the willpower to introduce myself to the man. But I later reached out to him through the right channels and he agreed we should meet for coffee and discuss the important things in life: literature.

Rick, too, had met Jay, and they'd become good buddies. Jay was the cement that Rick and I had stepped in before it had dried. Now we were stuck together.

When I got off the train, a man with striking blue eyes begged to borrow my phone so he could call his caseworker. I reluctantly handed it over, hearing my mother's warnings like a fork on a plate between my ears. The man paced up and down, screaming into my phone. When he finished with the call, he handed my phone back, his face splitting into a Cheshire cat grin. Relieved that he hadn't run off with it—or tried to stab me—I headed up the escalator.

I recognised Rick immediately, waiting on the station steps, and strode over.

'We meet at last,' I said.

The man turned, holding his camera in two hands, and snapped a photo of me. I blinked.

'How was the ride up?' he asked.

'I'm just glad there weren't any bus replacements.' I wiped the sweat from under my curls. 'They've been happening all month. You know, this one time I got on the wrong replacement bus and somehow ended up in Altona. I slept on the beach that night.' I was starting to ramble again. And despite my consciousness of it, I couldn't stop myself. 'Oh, the other day there was this old bloke sitting right where you're standing. He was grumbling to himself: *those fuckers stole my Bacardi while I was asleep!* They could've at least left a man to his good taste.'

Rick didn't say much. I feared I'd already started to bore him. Why couldn't I just turn off my mouth and play it cool?

He broke the silence with: 'So how do you know Jay?'

'Well ... he does the street letters, I do the street poems. It was bound to happen eventually, right?'

'The street seems to bring all kinds of people together.' He grinned and put his camera away. 'Where is the bastard, anyway?'

A hand slapped me on the back.

It was Jay.

'Should we hit the State Library?'

The three of us ambled away.

RICK WALKOW

Johnny turned jumpy when we got to the State Library. He talked like a jagged telegraph machine:

'Yeah … yeah! I guess that could work. And that right there at the steps. You want to sit down here? Sure! Let's sit down here on this bench. Woah! The day's beautiful. It's just …'

When he was babbling, I looked across the lawn. The building was beautiful. It was weird to think that I used to study there every weekend when I was younger. After a few laps around a giant tree, a flock of pigeons gathered on the green branches, their movements disturbing the spotted shades.

Johnny looked at the library. My attention was fixed on a kid under the tree full of pigeons. He looked at them and said, 'Stop! All of you! Stop! Stop looking at me like that!'

Johnny noticed the kid too. 'You think those birds will shit on him?'

'I hope so,' I said and turned to Johnny.

'But still, isn't it ridiculous that we met over a photo?' He turned to me with a big grin on his face. 'I probably looked super edgy and all when I was smoking. Then I recognised you and … well, I couldn't do it.'

'I don't bite,' I said. 'You know that was also the day I left my job?'

'Really?' He raised his brow.

The kid paced under the branches. Then he flinched and I

46

saw a gooey yellow patch on his shoulder. He screamed 'Mum!' and ran away. Johnny and I chuckled.

We saw Jay wandering around the library's grounds. 'I don't know what circle he runs in,' I said.

'I'm still getting the hang of him.' Johnny shrugged. 'Why is he looking at that phone booth?'

JAY KHAN

The sun was rising, the city was waking, and so was I. A crooked old man with a grey beard stood beside a telephone booth, sifting through his oversized plastic bag with anxious and impatient fingers. His bag, dumped on the floor beside his feet, made from multi-coloured fabric, contained ripped and stained cardboard. There was a name, painted on the front of his bag:

GREG

I watched him shuffle his feet from left to right, look up and down, curse under his breath as if the cardboard told him ugly, ugly words.

'Shit!' he yelled with a gruff Italian accent. 'I found you!'

His head popped out from inside his oversized bag, along with a little white slip of paper. He held it against his eyes like a pair of glasses and started mashing numbers into the payphone keys. 'Hello! Hello!' he yelled into the phone without paying the caller fee. 'I'm here. I'm here! Why aren't you talking? Hello! Hello!'

The man threw the phone at the holder, causing the

beeeeeeeep ringtone to echo from the hanging phone. He jumped on the spot, shaking his fists, and yelled at Rick and Johnny sitting on a stone step nearby. 'Why you looking at me? Why, why? You can't sit there ... you shouldn't sit on stone or steel! Unless you want your asshole to fall out and bleed dry. Oh, and you can't eat chocolate and meat. Because it's bad for your kidneys! You hear me!?'

'Is that right?' I said, stepping in.

He turned to look at me and shouted, 'For hell, it is.' As if he expected God to hear him. 'That's why I carry this cardboard with me. People think I'm crazy when they hear my advice, but I'm not. I know I'm not. I'm just careful. Like Jesus, before he got crucified. That's all. But still, people don't believe me. But when they get old, and their asshole falls out, they sure as hell wish they listened to me. I know six people who should have listened to me. They got a hanging asshole for the rest of their life now! Huh ...'

JOHNNY LOCK

I wrote a few lines in my notebook, sitting there watching Jay navigate this strange conversation with a man named Greg, in front of a telephone box covered in greasy handprints.

Those lines became a poem.

THE CARDBOARD MAN

Gregory the Sicilian preaches,
  emerging from the telephone box
    like a storybook pop-up

'Stone and steel,' he preaches
  somehow making more sense
    than my rambling Nonno

He preaches a cardboard seat
  or a whole cinema of them
    in a frayed bag on his back

We can't sit here apparently:
  not because he's claimed it
    but for the truth he preaches

If we ignore what he preaches
  we accept promises of a bleeding rear
    and our future seatlessness

I make no move to stand,
  writing my rear a death sentence
    in rejection of his preaches

'I am a learner,' Preacher Greg preaches
  of meat and chocolate
    like drill-bits for your kidneys

then my kidneys are holy.

RICK WALKOW

The conversation with Greg was over and we went back into the streets holding our asses. We passed a few convenience stores and ended up in front of a bank. Jay stopped dead in his tracks. I thought he had found a coin on the floor, but he turned and looked at me with wide blue eyes.

'You know who's more of an ass?' He gestured at a bald monk in an orange puffer jacket. 'Don't … don't look …' But it was too late.

The monk's face lit up and he stopped the three of us in our tracks and said, 'Eh-hey! Have you ever considered Buddhism, my friends?' He had a German accent.

'Er … not particularly,' Jay said and looked at the book in the monk's hands.

'Do you read?'

'No. It hurts my head,' Jay replied.

'That's alright.' The monk had one of those smiles that would piss off any depressed person. The kind of smile you know you couldn't obtain in this day and age as a sane person. 'I'm just trying to spread peace, which will help ease your pain …'

The passing crowd faded in and out and we stood still with the man in the orange jacket, listening to his sermons. 'You can buy this book on donation and you can learn all about meditation.'

Then and there, an ambulance stopped on the other side of the street, in front of an adult video store. A homeless man was convulsing on the floor and by the looks of it, he'd overdosed.

'By the way, this is the way we can spread peace …' the monk said. 'You see, I run these meditation workshops and …'

The medical staff and the police cars pulled over and a nurse administered CPR to the overdosed man. They brought out a stretcher and pulled the guy up into the ambulance. The doors closed tight, and not a trace of what had happened was left in the streets.

'We need to clear out all the miseries of the world …'

The monk eyed the ambulance and started giggling as the siren faded.

Jay looked at Johnny and I, and murmured, 'what the fuck?'

'So yeah,' the monk continued. 'If you want to try it out, make sure you get on the right journey, so you're not bothered by suffering.'

JAY KHAN

We walked off. Trams passed by. Pigeons shat on the pavement. I turned to look at my hands, red like my mood. 'I call that guy the monk made from money,' I muttered to the boys, missing eye contact. 'He's always hustling, hustling, hustling for a dollar on the corner of Swanston Street, where the fiends of the night go bump in the light.'

'Bump in the light?' Rick asked. 'I don't get it …'

'Too bad. You missed out. Anyways, that prick is always wearing the same old orange getup with no shoes, asking people to read his book at the cost of a small donation. Promising enlightenment with every purchase. Motherfucker. Did you hear what he said when I asked him if he'd helped people today?'

The thought of the monk's *serine* (made-up word to express anger) smile made me madder and madder. My fingers clenched. My asshole tightened. There's nothing more that annoys me in this world than the sight of religious salespeople. Twisting people's insecurities into a fast buck. Wankers of a first degree.

'He didn't know what to say, did he? He just smiled all twisted like he always does and asked Johnny to buy that bloody book, because apparently reading that book is the only way to be a good person. Who's he to tell me what good and bad is? He's hustling people for a dollar every day, selling strangers fake promises. He needs to look in the mirror and grow some hair.'

Johnny laughed and got Rick going too.

'And that man … that man lying unconscious on the floor, shaking violently, frothing at the mouth, overdosing on crystal junk. That monk guy didn't give a shit about him. All he cared about was the money he's going to pillage from Johnny. That asshole selling karma on the street.'

Rick continued giggling, latching onto the rage that spilled from my mouth.

I decided to drop it and closed my eyes. But there he was again, in my mind. The bloody monk man with no shoes, standing on a pile of injured, overdosing bodies as the sirens wailed. GNEE! GNAW! GNEE! GNAW! A smile dribbled from his face as he howled with laughter over passing strangers. 'Ha-hA-Ha-hA! Buy my book, buy my book! Ha-hA-Ha-hA!'

JOHNNY LOCK

It certainly seemed to be the day for poetry. Jay had led Rick and I up and down so many different streets that I had no idea where the train station was. There was a new strange character on every corner and my notebook loved them. I filled it with sketches of their faces or notes about their quirks. I tended to try to make sense of every encounter I had by writing down a few lines that came to mind, or recording the words I heard exchanged, and then experimented with writing a poem out of what I'd seen and felt.

Rick glanced over my shoulder and moved his lips as he read over the stanzas.

'Did you just write this now?' he asked.

I nodded. 'Yeah. It's about that monk.'

Jay's ears pricked up. 'You wrote about the monk? Go on. Read it, Johnny.'

I looked around. The faces of the people passing us by in the street looked three times larger, like bulbous caricatures taunting me. The pedestrian lights blinked. Cars honked their horns. A baby was crying somewhere.

'What? Read it … here?'

'Go on,' said Jay. 'And don't whisper. Shout it so all the motherfucking monks in Tibet can hear it.'

PHILIPP

The monk's name is Philipp
and Philipp's smile should unnerve me,
   instead it fills today's void
   with the Bhagavad Gita
ensnaring me for a moment

and a moment more ...

holding me ...

so long ...

I miss the ambulance
pulling up outside Club X

Philipp the Monk talks about suffering
   but fails to see the suffering man
on the pavement of Swanston Street;
his eyes are wide awake with life,
in ignorance
   of the closeness of death

is he ignorant on purpose?
  or does he blame the sufferer?

RICK WALKOW

Dust settled on the streets and we were tired from all the running around. After circling the streets over and over, we ended up in a side alley prefaced by a menu stand with a French flag attached to it. The tables, aligned under the eaves, were mostly empty. We sat down at one of them, but no one came to our aid. I leaned back in my chair and shuffled my eyes from Johnny to Jay. People who write together usually start from a humble place. Sometimes it was the backlot of a theatre or after a university class. For the three of us, it was at a little cafe where French tunes echoed against two buildings.

And the street itself had its own kind of rhythm. At our seats looking into the street, strange whispers seeped through the looming french tunes. From the grunts of the hunch-backed preacher covering his rear from concrete slabs, to the clatter of coins in the monk's pocket, his face frozen in joy at the sight of pain. We heard and saw them all, imprinting those details onto our paper tapes.

'There's a tale to this city,' Jay said, 'and I'll find it. Believe me, I'll find it …' He sprang from his seat. 'Ready to hit the streets again?'

Johnny and I trailed his steps, dashing off with him to another stranger, into another strange world of noises; into haunted visions and the endless toils between mercy and callousness.

GHOST OF GONZO

RICK WALKOW

Lauren came over with an iced long black.

'Here you go.' She looked out of the window. 'You're not heading out today, are you?'

The morning was already unbearable, but the heat was far from peaking. The train pulled in and I saw the announcer through the window, wiping his forehead with a handkerchief.

'Attention all passengers. Your next service to Flinders Street will depart in ten minutes on platform two.'

Business people lost their ties and blazers because the heat was brewing their murderous tempers. Their brows were screwed tight.

'This will keep me going.' I drained the long black.

'You're mad,' Lauren said.

I smiled and slung my bag over my shoulder, heading for the door. 'In a bit.' Lauren shook her head.

'Good morning, sir.'

The announcer walked up to the train door, sweat rolling down his cheeks. 'Enjoy the aircon while you can. Bad day for a trip.' He pressed the button on the carriage door.

'Thank you.'

I walked in and all of the passengers were floating ghosts, wandering from one air-conditioned box to the next, glued to their screens. The train raced through the emerging heat, brightening at each stop. At Flinders Street, all the ghosts arose at once, drifting awake as they floated onto the platform. I followed their flow, watching them scatter on the upper platform, until I was completely alone.

Moments later, a hand landed on my shoulder. I whipped my head back to see Johnny in what he called his 'summer wear'.

JOHNNY LOCK

It was a sweltering day. The peak of summer. I wasn't dressed for the weather, wearing long stripes underneath a black tee that clung tight to my body. Rick looked me up and down.

'What the hell are you wearing? Did you look at the weather chart today?'

'You really think it will get to forty?' I asked, shuddering. 'Maybe the meteorologists are lying.'

'The heat will probably pick up later,' Rick said. 'You're gonna die.'

'We'll see.' I rubbed my palms together. My mother seemed to think I was going to get heatstroke in my stripes. But I preferred to hide, to shrink inside myself, so that no one could see the me within—the me concealed, a walking secret.

'I hope we don't have another Black Summer.'

'The bushfires from last year?' Rick asked.

'Unsettling name for it. That's the problem with Australia. Fire. You leave a half-burnt cigarette on the ground and—boom— wildfire. If you don't backburn throughout the year, summer hits

and you're fucked.' I took a deep breath. 'My dad's street burned
to ashes in a bushfire a few years ago, you know?'

Rick looked away at a man balancing a milk crate on his
head.

Jay arrived as if he'd just crawled out of the grave. 'Look what the
cat dragged in.' I gawked at him. 'Have you been gravedigging all
night?'

'You look like shit,' Rick said.

Jay scratched his stubble. 'I was up doing stuff last night.
Just …' He shrugged us off. 'I need a fucking coffee.'

'Isn't that just standard procedure at this point?' I asked.

We found a side-street coffee stand and placed our orders. A
gaunt man in a cap, with disappointment in the creases of his face,
stumbled into line cradling a coffee cup.

'Look at that guy.' I nudged Rick. 'He hasn't even finished
his first cup and he already needs another.'

'I can relate,' Rick said.

The man looked over his shoulder at us. He had blistered lips
and bright blue eyes, those eyes Jay and I noticed everywhere.

JAY KHAN

'People don't carry help anymore,' the man mumbled to himself.
Catching our eyes, he redirected his mumblings. 'It's getting harder
and harder every day. To find some help. You know what I mean?'
he said. As if we knew.

    'People don't carry coins or cash anymore. Where's
the help? Huh? Where's it gone? The world's becoming
crueller and crueller by thedaythehourtheminute. Hell,
I can't keep up. Why does society have to keep moving
forwardandforwardandforwardandforward? Only to leave people
behind? Like me. And the others out here on the street, trying to
catch up at a pace too slow to ever know. Where's the help? Huh?
Where's it gone? Nobody carries cash anymore … or coins … or
their attention. All I want is three meals a day, or a nice chat to
make me feel human. Is that too much to ask? Huh? Is it? Where's
the help?'

    His voice trailed off, back into his inner mumblings.

    'Where's the help?'

JOHNNY LOCK

Jay went up to the stand and bought the man with blue eyes
a croissant. Had Jay read my mind? I'd wanted to buy him a
croissant too, after I saw him eyeing one off in the window. I didn't
want to be a saviour. But I was a sucker for a good smile. Was it
more wrong for me to offer him one, or to leave him be, while I
sipped my coffee and watched him mumble about his misfortune?

The man lumbered away juggling two coffees and a
croissant, but his grievances replayed like a nervous stutter in the
alley of my mind.

*'All I want is three meals a day. Or a nice chat to make me
feel human.'*

'That was kind of you,' I said to Jay.

Jay looked away. 'Shut up.'

Down another lane, an elderly man on a milk crate was calling out
to passersby, balancing a stack of magazines on his lap. 'Take it
easy! Take it easy!'

The vendor caught me looking at him. He knew. He knew I
wanted to buy a copy of *The Big Issue* by the way I licked my lips.
My hand reached for my wallet and his toothy grin unveiled itself.
He charged me $9. Dolly Parton looked pleased with herself on the
front cover (and on pages 12–17).

Another man approached the vendor after me. 'Aren't they
$5?' he asked.

'$5?' The vendor leaned back and screwed up his face. 'Where did you pull that out of? Your asshole? What are you playing at?'

The man bought one anyway.

I pointed out an orange poster on the alley wall. It was a hazy image of a straight-postured woman meditating. I thought about my experience with meditation. Why didn't more people do it? Maybe they lacked the patience. Maybe it didn't work like medicine for everyone.

Rick grunted. 'I've seen Buddhist flyers all over the damn place today.'

'I noticed that too,' Jay said. 'Did I tell you guys that I'm going to a meditation retreat? The place is in Tasmania. I'll be gone for a while.'

Rick and I exchanged glances.

'You're ... what?' I asked.

Rick seemed unimpressed. 'You're the last person I'd expect to go on a meditation retreat.'

'Echo wanted to go, so I said fuck it. I'm worried that if I don't go with her, she'll have a revelation that I'm a wanker and leave me.'

'That girl loves you. She won't leave,' I said.

'Yeah, well.' Jay's eyes swept from the meditation poster to the sparkling shards of glass in the gutter. 'Going deep into yourself can do crazy things to you, man. I'd be lying if I said I'm not scared like a motherfucker.'

I slapped him on the back. 'You'll come back a changed man. You'll be like that quack monk made from money.'

'Or more likely,' Rick said, 'a madman.'

'A lunatic,' I added.

'A nut.'

'I'm already mad,' Jay laughed. 'Now shut up. Let's get some stories.'

And the three of us returned to the streets, capturing the tales everyone missed, giggling amidst the strangeness of it all. The alley darkness morphed into blinding heavenly light. We shielded our eyes and complained about the heat, the way everyone in Melbourne did.

RICK WALKOW

I had spent the better part of my childhood as a bookworm. My shelf was lined with everything from RL Stein's novels to Star Wars comics. Then I got older and fell into the rabbit hole of Twain and Hemingway. I couldn't live without books, so I dragged Jay and Johnny down to Dymocks. After browsing around for a bit, I spotted a copy of Hunter S Thompson's *The Rum Diary*.

'Don't you already have a fucking stack you need to get through?' Jay said. He was right because there was in fact a fucking stack on my nightstand. He was finally the voice of reason amidst all his madness, but I shut my ears and flipped the book to the first page.

'You know I've been there right?' Jay pointed at the page, printed: *San Juan, Winter of 1958.*

I turned to him. 'Really?'

'I went there on a plane to see a girl I thought I loved.'

Jay had that mad smile again. 'But halfway through the trip, she cancelled on me. And when I got into the cab, the driver kidnapped me.'

Johnny corked his head. 'Kidnapped?'

'I had to jump out of a moving car. Then the guy tried to run me over.'

And that's the kind of gonzo Jay was.

I bought the book and the three of us walked out of the store. Johnny and I sat on a bench at a road's junction, while Jay paced in circles under the scorching sun. 'Do you see that man in an army uniform?' he asked. 'Do you see him?'

'Yeah?' I ignored him to read my new book. But when I lifted my head he was gone.

'Well.' Johnny looked at me. 'Off he goes again.'

JAY KHAN

The sun beat down, hard and hurtful on the back of my neck when I saw Army Steve sitting alone on a green milk crate under a canopy outside 7-Eleven, smoking a four dollar cigarette in his brown camo-gear, flaunting the Australian flag on both hat and heart. I'd seen Steve on the street before, yet I'd never heard a word leave his mouth. I guess I never needed to. Because one look in those big blue eyes of his told a story so cruel, so ghoulish, that even the strangest of strange hearts would turn ice-cold to the core.

You know, he knows, you know, he's seen some shit in the killing fields that drove him out of society and its rigid ways.

64

And there was the Gremlin. An aged white man so burnt by the sun his skin was as cured as leather. His mouth dribbled black and rotten. He had demonic markings indented into his face and body. 666 carved across his chest. Pentagram carved into his back. A staple creature going bump in the light, clearly in sight, around Swanston Street. Always cursing, cursing, cursing the world around him, punching and spitting at invisible angels in the face.

The Gremlin hobbled over to Army Steve, screaming, 'Grrrrrrr! Grrrr! Arrrrrr!'

Army Steve rubbed the Gremlin's shoulder gently, as if they were brothers from a long-lost time when they still had their sanity.

And then, when Army Steve stubbed his ciggie onto the simmering concrete and walked away, leaving the Gremlin to fight his invisible angels alone, it hit me.

Could it be they went to war together, all those years ago? And could it be, that only one of the two came back with a functional mind and a mouthful of teeth, while the other returned so wartorn and scarred that he forgot his own name?

Maybe whatever was left of the human in the Gremlin died at war. And maybe Army Steve was the man that dragged the Gremlin's disfigured body back to this city.

JOHNNY LOCK

We walked along Swanston Street for the tenth time that scorching afternoon. It amazed me how I hadn't collapsed. Jay pointed to a sickly-looking man covered in scarified tattoos, waiting at a pedestrian light.

    'He's an interesting character, don't you think?' he asked.

    'The scarified skeleton,' I said.

    He looked at me, eyes blazing. 'If you don't write a poem about him, I'm going to be fucking mad.'

    I sat down on a bench, took out my notebook and wrote the first stanza.

THE SCARIFIED SKELETON

The scarified skeleton
walks like Santa out-of-work,
   when the world lost
its belief in his magic,
in his gifts—
   I wonder why I always
loved to believe?
   I still do and everyone knows;
   even when
the cynics weigh me down,
I believe in everything.

The cynics, too, weigh down
Santa with his scars:
   he falls south.
His back is a sad canvas
of surface-raised pain,
which he'll carry
to the street grave
   between
a graffiti wall
   and
a stickered skip.

But on the hottest day,
his age-old scars open up again,
and he dreams of northern snows
and the gifts he no longer has to give—
   but all he has
are city snows,
and the city snows
won't cut it.

RICK WALKOW

Everyone in the city was in a bad temper. Babies cried in prams
and yuppies in suits grunted the same muted grunt whenever they
bumped into each other at the intersection. I was on the edge of
strangling myself, because it was an easier way out than breathing
that stifling air. We stopped in front of McDonald's to steal some
cool air. A guy with a broom came around:

'You! The three of you. What the hell are you doing at the
door?'

I said nothing. Jay and Johnny looked into the streets like
they were searching for something. A half-naked man rode past
the storefront on a bicycle, spilling water over himself when he
stopped at a traffic light. The light turned green and the broom guy
continued:

'Stop blocking the door! Get the hell out of here!'

The three of us ended up in the miserable heat again.

'I just can't be fucked,' Jay said. 'What is it with people in
this city?'

'You're the dumbass by default if you ever come into the
city,' I said and wiped my forehead.

'It's the same thing with the dickhead artists over here,' he
said. 'I messaged so many of them, but none of them wanted to
meet. It's like I'm talking at a wall!'

Johnny reached for a cigarette but didn't light it. 'Do you

think we actually need these people around?'

'We don't.' Jay ruffled his hair. 'We need to start something here. Something they've never seen before. What's there to lose?'

For Johnny and I, Jay was the key into a crazy underworld hidden away from our familiar views. It helped that he wasn't actually from Melbourne, so that he was able to see everything with a fresh pair of eyes. I called him a 'mad cat' and we were the same kind of mad, but he was a different kind of courageous.

JAY KHAN

BEAM! BOOM! SIZZLE! BURN! Since the sun had been beating down all day with unforgiving cancerous rays, we decided to take refuge under the shadow of a towering concrete skyscraper on the corner of Lonsdale Street, hoping, begging, to find forgiveness in the cool, cool shade. After collapsing onto the floor, Rick dropped his shoulders, stared at his cold unopened Coca-Cola, and began swaying from side to side. Johnny clenched his eyes. His chest moved up, down, like an injured animal, looking as if he was a few degrees from death in that thick striped shirt of his.

'Why the hell would you wear that on a day like this?' I groaned under my breath.

Rick and Johnny, too far gone to notice my question, watched strangers stumble in and out of focus, wiping great deals of salty sweat from their dragging eyes. Four shirtless fat men waddled in a group, with their hands on their heads, huffing, puffing from the heat of the day.

Ruffling through my fraying blue backpack, I slurred, 'Hey Johnny, hold on to this.' Wiping trenches of sweat from in-between my eyes. 'Catch!'

A pair of hot and sweaty scissors flew from my hand.

Johnny screeched, waving his wet hand in pain. 'What the hell?'

I reached over to pick up the scissors. 'Sorry mate. I thought you could catch. Besides, you aren't bleeding.'

Rick giggled, holding the cold Coca-Cola to his head.

'Here,' I said, delicately passing Johnny a roll of sellotape and a pair of scissors. 'Hold on to these please, will ya?'

The sun rose above the skyscraper. The shade crept closer. I pulled out a crumpled white A4 sheet of paper from my bag. Straightened it out, stood up, and tried to find a spot to post it.

'Hey, Johnny, can you give me a hand posting the letter, mate? It's a bitch to post on my own. The sellotape keeps splitting every time I tear a piece.'

Johnny slowly and hurtfully stood up. 'Sure.'

CUT! PULL! TAPE! CUT! PULL! TAPE!

'There, how about that?' I said. Stepping out of the shade to read the letter.

Dear Stranger,

I feel like a diagnosed stranger,
    who belongs to no one and nowhere.
All the time, wherever I go.
A jigsaw piece for the wrong puzzle. A circle for a square hole.

My mind, my heart, my feet, are constantly running
    from who I ought to be.
So people no longer see a stranger in me.

For a year I've been knocking from door to door
    hoping to see what Melbourne can offer me.
As if I'm some sort of phantom, flickering like an old film,
    floating through scenes, unnoticed.
Knocking, knocking, knocking on a different artist's door,
    only to hear the echo of my own knock.
But when the door does open,
    the first line is always the same.
'What do you want? What can you give me?'
I rarely drink. Nor do drugs.
So to them, I can't give them the gratification of intoxication,
    which apparently will make a masterpiece. In their minds.
And when the door slams shut, ice ice cold, in the hot, hot sun,
    I look on through the letter box and peek on through
    to the other side,
    imagining myself amidst a crowd of creatives,
    amidst their rambling ideologies,
    spurting jibba-jabba ab-nabs as if they hold the words of God.

I stand there, among a crowd of 'forward thinking' people,
    feeling more lonely and backwards than I did
    standing behind the door. All alone.
So I slip back out, in my head,
    through the letterbox, back to my body,
    and wander on through the streets.

Feeling like a diagnosed stranger,
  who belongs to no one and nowhere.
Scribbling down stories nobody wants to see,
  because I'm sure,
  the stories feel like me.
So I place them
  anyways,
  across the walls,
  for all the other diagnosed strangers to see.

Rick, stumbling to his feet, cracking open the Coca-Cola, read the letter and said, 'Jay … that's not depressing at all ...'

'What do you mean?'

'I mean, it's good and all … but did you really feel like that?'

'Yeah … before you two came along ...'

The shade crawled closer and closer to our toes.

'Nobody in this city wanted to meet me. I felt like the whole world was closing in on me faster than this bloody shade. Everywhere I went, I felt as if people were watching me, judging me, wishing I never existed. That's how I got to know the street so well. It's the only place where people gave me the time of the day without giving me those eyes. Not like those fucking artists who call themselves open-minded … I remember when I first arrived here, when I went to a club alone ...'

'You went to a club alone?' Johnny asked as if my statement was unspeakable.

'Back in Berlin, I always used to club alone, it was a ritual of mine. The only place I could close my eyes, dance, and forget about the world. But when I did it here, people literally laughed me out of the club. It really fucked me up. And one time when I walked down Fitzroy (a hipster area) a group of people laughed at the way I walked, with my hands behind my back. They called me *grandpa cunt*. Everything I did back then felt wrong, strange, not cool enough. So I fell into this sort of downhill spiral where I lost all of my confidence. A part of me died. I felt so alone … so worthless … in a city so far from home.

'But when I found the street and started posting my letters across its walls, a new part of me was born. Something more punk, more aggressive. Now I don't give a shit about those people who call themselves artists. Or whatever the fuck they think they are. Now I just want to focus on creating, so I can stick my middle fingers in their ears and yell, look! I don't need you! This is what you missed! Dickheads!

'So, yeah, I guess the story is a little depressing, but maybe other people might have felt the way I did, before meeting you two.'

'I've never felt the need to contact any artists,' Rick said. 'I'm too busy with my own shit to worry about anyone else. Most artists and writers are a bunch of quacks. They talk too much, create too little.'

Johnny, still in a daze and holding his chest with clenched eyes, murmured, 'Boys, can we find some aircon to cool off? I'm not feeling so good. I feel dizzy, my chest hurts …'

RICK WALKOW

The heat drove a fever of madness into Johnny's mind. When we walked through the streets he slapped a postal box here and kicked a bin there while rambling absolute nonsense like those strangers on the streets.

I turned to him and stopped him from picking up a cigarette butt on the ground. 'You good?'

'No! This heat is just ... ergh!' And off he went on another string of broken depressive rambles Jay liked to call 'jibba-jabba'. I tuned in and out. Eventually, Johnny stopped me in my tracks at a junction and punched my shoulder. 'Earth to Rick. Did you hear anything we said?'

'No.' I looked across the road at the entrance of an arcade. 'We need to get you some air-conditioning to shut you up.'

'You're melting our damn minds,' Jay sighed.

The traffic light turned green and the two of them followed me across the road. I rushed into the arcade to take a hit of cold air. We passed a line of clothing stores with ugly coats. Then something caught my eye in one of the windows. Under the dim tungsten bulbs, a dead owl looked at me like I owed it money.

'Hey, you two.' I stopped in front of the taxidermy store. 'Look at this ...'

Johnny ran up beside me to look into the window. 'That looks like my Nonno's bakery.'

'Is your grandpa making bread with dead animals?' I said.

'If so, I'm breaking into his bakery.' I turned around to punch Jay on the shoulder but he wasn't there. He was in a daze, cursing at himself, far behind, lagging in the heat. I shrugged and went into the store.

There was no one at the counter. There were skeletons of bats, lizards in frames, and a rat standing upright, frozen in its death stare. I browsed around, turned the corner, and bumped into a dusty guy in a heavy tweed blazer. He didn't look that old, but he liked to pretend he was ancient and dusty. We held eyes for a second. The first thing that came out of my mouth was:

'Is this your store?'

'Mhm.' He signalled me to get out of his way.

'Don't you feel like a serial killer, living in a place like this?'

'I don't live here.' He sounded annoyed. I stood clear of his way. He went to the counter and sat down, making one of those 'ah!' noises when his ass landed on the cushion.

I went up to the counter. The man glanced up with those annoyed eyes. 'What do you want?'

'Just browsing.' I noticed the skeleton at the entrance of the store. It was a full-sized replica. I pointed at it and asked, 'Do you ever get lonely here at night?'

The guy raised his brows. 'What the hell do you want?'

'I was just wondering if you ever get lonely here at night.'

He opened one of the books on the counter and pretended to read it. 'Whoever you are, please go annoy someone else.'

I looked at the counter. 'Is that a skull?'

He rolled his eyes. 'Yes …'

'How much is it?'

'Three-hundred dollars.' He said it with one of those twangs that meant: *I know you can't afford it.*

'Why is it so expensive?' I asked while laying my hand on the skull. It felt like the real deal. All medieval scholars had skulls on their desks to remind themselves how short life was. I didn't want one for any noble reasons, no. I wanted one because I wanted one. I wanted to prop a skull on my desk in the middle of the night, so I could stare into its empty eye sockets and shout: *what the hell are you looking at?'*

'It's three-hundred dollars. Take it or leave it.' He returned to his book and I knew if I asked one more question, he'd throw the book in my face.

'I'll come back for it,' I said. 'You just wait. I'll be back.'

On my way out, I patted the full-sized skeleton on its shoulder. The owner sprang out of his seat, slammed his book, and yelled, 'Don't touch it!'

The entire store shook. The owl in the window fell off its perch.

JOHNNY LOCK

Something came over me and my jitters had turned into fatigue. I was minutes from total collapse. My neck was a string and my head hung from it like a Christmas bauble.

'Is caffeine a good idea?' I asked, then answered myself: 'I think coffee is a very good idea right now.'

Rick nudged me and I nearly fell over, saved only by a street pole that I clung to for support. 'It's a terrible idea,' he said.

'You're a mess.'

'If I don't … get any caffeine in me,' I slurred, 'I'm gonna ... fall asleep … on the pavement.'

'Then do it,' Jay said. 'Sleep, right here, right now on the footpath.'

'Will you make sure no one tramples on me?'

Jay and Rick laughed between them. 'We'll make sure everyone tramples on you,' Jay said. 'Come on, let's get you a coffee or something.'

'And some food,' I said. 'I'm going to be a zombie without energy.'

We found a convenience store. Jay saw Philipp, the monk with money, and left to talk to him. I went into the store and bought a Red Bull in a half-daze, avoiding the cashier's eyes and on the edge of falling asleep on the spot. He handed me the change and I stepped out of the store.

A man in a shabby coat saw me holding my wallet.

'Got a coin?' he asked. He had a palmful of coins and was working his way up the street to make it heavier.

I never carried change on me, but I had some at that moment. So I fished in my wallet to give him a dollar coin. The man spotted the $5 and $10 notes I had. His bloodshot eyes lit up. 'I'll give you these coins for a note,' he drawled. 'Please …'

Rick grabbed my shoulder. 'No.'

'Please … I'll give you these coins …'

I reached for the $5 note.

'Johnny. What the hell, man? No.'

I handed the shabby man the purple note. He licked his teeth and stared into my wallet. 'No, no, the ten, give me the ten. I'll give you these coins …'

There wasn't a bit of energy in me to refuse him. I would have given him my whole wallet without putting up a fight.

His free hand reached for my wrist. 'Come on, the ten … just give me the ten …'

Rick's grip clamped around my arm and dragged me back against my will. 'Come on,' he huffed.

Jay was still talking to the monk with money. I stood by and tried to listen in, but my focus dipped in and out. I sat down on a bench and tried to gather myself, my hands shaking, eyes drooping, head hanging. I cracked open the can, took a sip and sighed with relief.

'I hope this helps,' I told Rick. 'I don't know what happened to me. Maybe it's the heat. Maybe it's my classes. Maybe it's all of it. It's all draining the fucking life out of me.'

'You should quit,' Rick said. 'You've read too much. Don't be like those dickheads.'

'Maybe.' I took another sip.

I was starting to feel awake again. We saw the man who was chasing help from earlier that day. I remembered his mumbling.

'No one carries help in their pockets anymore … all I want is enough money to hit up McDonald's.'

He recognised us from before and his face split into a wicked grin. 'I got it! I got my help!' He'd found it in the form of a $5 note that he waved around like a winning lottery ticket.

'Way to go, mate,' I said as we walked by him and I threw my Red Bull can in the bin.

'Time for McDonald's!'

JAY KHAN

The sun's rays turned tame after being swallowed by a cloud of
night. Johnny, no longer a few degrees from death, looked at his
hand with a smile, holding five newly written poems. Rick walked
by my side, looking sad, as if this was the end to something.
Passing trams lit something up in his eyes that I recognised in the
mirror months ago. A strange sort of change. From the street.

We wandered, still sweating as a group of three, with closed
notebooks, slurping 7-Eleven coffees. We wandered and wandered
and wandered through cool, quiet streets one last time, before
heading back to our old lonely ways for an undetermined amount
of time.

When passing the State Library garden, Johnny pointed
out the man who needed help. Now shirtless, in his boxer shorts,
snoring, fast asleep. Crumpled McDonald's bags clumped into a
pillow. Thick leftover Buddhism leaflets were scattered beside his
body, across the lawn.

Johnny picked up a leaflet and said, 'Jay, whatever you do,
don't let them turn you into Phillip.'

I laughed, thinking of his *serine* smile. 'Don't worry, I'm not
easily brainwashed.'

Pigeons in droves flew past us. Blinding our vision with
a flash of dirty white. A lady, wearing great big fluffy earmuffs,
emptied a cement-sack of breadcrumbs onto the floor. Birds swept

up the bread like locusts in a corn field. A police car, blaring a siren, drove past. The lady grabbed hold of her earmuffs and crouched on the floor, screaming, 'Aghhhh!'

Rick asked me, 'You are coming back, right?'

I looked at the leaflet in Johnny's hands. *FOLLOW BUDDHA TO ENLIGHTENMENT.* And said, 'I think so ...'

Johnny threw the leaflet onto the floor, stamped on it, twisted his foot, smothered it with dirt and said, 'I'm not very good at goodbyes. So I'm just going to leave. See you when you're back, Jay. Yeah?'

Rick nodded. 'Yeah ...'

And before I could say 'Yeah?' in return. The two of them walked off, through and through the street, as a pair, back to their suburban white-picket fenced world. Far, far away from the street and its strange ways.

There's a tale to this city

CONCRETE FOREST

JAY KHAN

Ten people on a bus. Travelling to a forest. To find enlightenment. A firefighter with pinprick blonde hair and a strong square face looked at me. 'Are you ready?'

I looked at him, juddering from side to side, crammed inside a bus, riding up, up, up along some dirt road into some Tasmanian forest far from civilisation without a phone. 'Sure.'

Echo looked out of the window at all the passing trees, smiling, expecting a great change in her life over the next ten days.

A guy from California yelled over the engine, 'Everyone, I'm Frank! Did you know I'm going to save the world?'

The bus hit a stone. THUD! We all flew upwards. Frank hit his head.

'Have any of you done this before?' asked a frail-looking Hispanic man in the back.

Frank interrupted, 'Did you not hear me? I'm going to save the world. I'm leaving for Chile when this is over, to install solar panels. Good money over there. And I'm making the world a greener place.'

A Chinese businessman spoke from the front of the bus. 'I've done four of these. It's all about the eye.' Pointing to his upper lip, he yelled, 'Remember that.'

THUD! The bus hit another stone.

'What do we do when we get to the meditation place?' I asked.

The Chinese businessman coughed, 'Huh? You don't know?'

'No?'

'How did you get a spot on this bus?'

'I don't know.' I pointed at Echo. 'She dragged me here.'

'Dragged you?' yelled Frank. 'It's a privilege to be here!'

'Sure ...'

The Chinese businessman shouted over the hum of the diesel engine. 'I've seen so many people break down,' he said, 'They curl up in a ball and cry, they just can't take it. Some go home broken. My last retreat broke me. I hope this one will be better.'

Frank added, 'The CEO of my company did one and he said people started screaming and yelling after the third day.'

The Hispanic guy mumbled to himself, 'I'm just here for the free food ...'

The bus moved up, up, up, further into the middle of nowhere.

The bus arrived. We got out. Forest was everywhere. Big bushes, tall trees. Strange-looking spiders with red neon legs, the size of my palm.

'Everybody follow me with your bags,' spat the bus driver with a lisp, waddling to the meditation office, flaunting his hairy white bum-crack with every step. Echo looked at me and laughed. I returned the glance with forced laughter.

The meditation office blurred into view. A white office trailer with a sign hanging from the door: *Boys on the left. Girls on the right.* After stepping in, I said my goodbyes to Echo, split left, and sat down on a long table next to the frail Hispanic man. When he scratched his ear, I noticed a shiny brown bald patch on the crown of his head. Miniature multi-coloured Tibetan flags dangled from the brown hair around his patch like Nepalese Christmas ornaments. I said, 'Hello.' He smiled and twiddled his thumbs.

A lady walked in, shouting, 'Everybody listen up.' Pulling out a stack of papers from her oversized handbag. 'Here, I have your contracts. Before you sign, you need to know we will not take liability for your mental health, because how you handle this program is on you. The program is very effective and healthy for everybody if completed correctly, but if you leave before the tenth day, you may end up with permanent mental damage. By signing this form, you declare your mental health is not our liability.' The lady scratched her cotton-white hair and continued. 'You may have heard stories of people leaving mid-way through this program in a horrific mental state. They are most likely true, but worry not. If you sign this form and devote yourself to the full ten-day period, you will feel the true benefit of this retreat. The meditation program is designed to crack your mind open, bring all your worries and closeted skeletons to the surface, and let you dissolve them one by one. Any questions?'

Silence filled the air. The clock went TIK! TOK! TIK! TOK!

'Now then, before I pass the pens around, is there anyone here who wants to leave before we begin?'

The returning meditators smiled. The newcomers looked from left to right. My neighbour just wanted the free food.

'Nobody?' she repeated.

TIK! TOK! TIK! TOK!

'Okay, interesting … full house?' She passed the contracts around, shouting, 'From now on, talking is prohibited for the effectiveness of your path to enlightenment. You are no longer allowed to interact with the opposite sex or look at your neighbour. If you listen closely, I will call your name and Josh will guide you to your dorm.'

'Jay,' the leader shouted, 'Follow Josh to your dorm.'

I followed a man who looked like Jesus through the forest, his hair long and brown, his eyes unnaturally blue. An aura hovered around him so calm, so zen, he almost levitated to the white cabin in the woods. When we arrived, he said nothing and waved me off with one of those smiles that meant nothing. While unpacking my bags in the grey carpeted room with a bed and desk, I looked out of the window at kangaroos hopping into the bushes.

JOHNNY LOCK

I decided to give my hometown some love. The city was full of my poems—the alleys, the poles, the windows of shopfronts. But my hometown was bare, as if I'd never been there. I started at the park, sticking pieces up under a rotunda, on the playground, on the toilet stall doors. Then I made my way through the suburban streets, sticking them on every pole, tree and bus stop shelter I passed, like a dog marking its territory.

In my neighbourhood, there were always dogs barking. I turned a corner and was startled by a ferocious growl. A black dog sprang at me, clamped its teeth around my arm, drew blood. I fell onto the sidepath, knees grazing, vision blurry. My backpack fell in the grass. I wrestled the dog off me and rolled on the concrete.

Kicking my legs. Screaming. It pounced again, snarling in my face. Dribbling and spitting in my eyes. So I clenched them, hoping it would get rid of the pain. I wanted it painless. I didn't want to watch the thing maul me. Clenched. Clenched. Heard nothing.

I opened my eyes. There was no black dog. The concrete was beneath me. I was covered in sweat. Cars sped past, their drivers peering at me, through me, then returning to the road ahead.

'You all right, mate?'

A woman stared down at me, her eyebrows curving in. The bus shelter behind her looked like a blurry haze, a mirage. I cleared my throat and fixed my posture. 'Oh, yeah,' I said. 'Just … uh … meditating.'

We both knew I wasn't meditating. But she shrugged and returned to the bus shelter.

My heart was expanding and tightening in a fast, painful throb. I mopped the sweat on my face. *Maybe I should meditate. Maybe it will help. It's helped before.*

I took a deep breath in and thought of Jay in Tasmania. He was probably meditating at the same moment, only with more success and not on the side of the road. I tried to close my eyes, but had to open them to look around. To see if the black dog was back. I closed my eyes. A dog barked. Opened them. No dog. Closed them. A dog barked. Opened them. No dog.

It was hell. The last time I'd felt like that, I had been in Lakes Entrance. The motel I'd stayed at was on a cliffside overlooking the water. At first everything was going to plan. I stood on the lookout at 3 am, no shoes on. I stood totally still, took in the sights and smells of the summer night. Everything was so crisp. But when I tried to write in the motel room, my hands forgot how to bang on my typewriter. My eyes didn't know what I was looking at. I could hear wind rattling outside the motel room. Dogs barking. My heart threw itself around inside my ribs like a bird in a cage. And all that I'd managed to write was:

How can you dream?
How???
We just need to calm down somehow.
We know poems, not shaking, not lights …
not demons at the doors
HOUNDING TOO LOUD.

Another dog barked some way off. My head pounded. I closed my eyes and tried again, inhaled, exhaled, inhaled, exhaled. I heard the bus pull up, the doors open and the woman getting on. She murmured with the driver. Footfalls thudded. The driver. I felt his lingering gaze on me, then heard the doors close as the bus took off.

After settling down and resuming my poetry posting, I remembered another poem I'd written in Lakes Entrance, the morning after my breakdown:

Dawn is not impressed with me,
even if I am impressed by the dawn.

JAY KHAN

Day 1
4 am
(Toilet paper entries transcribed into narrative)

RING! RING! RING! My alarm beeps before dawn. DING!
DING! DING! Jesus hits a dong. THUD! THUD! Kangaroos hop
into hiding. Sleepy-eyed strangers silently weave in and out of
their dorms, rubbing their hands together, hoping to blow the cold
morning away. I stumble out of my dorm into darkness, blurry-
eyed, numb, cracking a twig with every step, following a trail of
torches to the meditation hall.

I walk into the hall, barefoot. The hall feels cold, dim, and dull.
Light-bars shine down onto the grey carpet beneath our feet,
shining like the sort of lights you'd expect to find in a funeral
home. White, bright, the sick sort of light. The room is split into
two. On one side, eleven men sit cross-legged on their assigned
cushions, eyes closed, upright, head down, three to a row, facing
north. On the other side, twelve women sit, looking much the
same.

    A milk-skinned man with an orange mole on his forehead
positions himself atop a white-cloth table in front of us, looking
down, wearing a white bed sheet. I sit down on my cushion and
wait for his instructions.

The man says nothing for an hour. He just sits there. So I stare at the surrounding strangers in the meantime, trying to make sense of the silence. Strangers bob their heads, up, down, up, down, looking as if they know something I don't. Eventually the mole-man pulls out a remote control and presses play.

A loud constipated groan erupts from a pair of speakers.

Grooooooaaaaaaannnnnnnnn!

Three old ladies in the front row vigorously bob their heads, up, down, up, down, murmuring to themselves.

Grooooooaaaaaaannnnnnnnn!

The man on the table stares at me with dead-fish blue eyes. He taps Jesus on the shoulder and sends him my way. Jesus arrives, draping his long hair over my shoulder, whispering, 'Jay. You need to close your eyes, you're distracting the others.' I close my eyes. He walks away.

Grooooooaaaaaaannnnnnnnn!

The ladies escalate their chanting. Heads bob up, down, all around. The mole-man scrunches his nose at me.

Grooooooaaaaaaannnnnnnnn!

Jesus turns around. I close my eyes before he can come over.

5:30 am

Another hour passes. The mole-man has still not said a word. I shift my bum from left to right, hoping to find comfort. My legs feel heavy. I look at Echo and find her meditating with closed eyes. I try to stare her down, flapping my hands discreetly, hoping she notices, but the mole-man sends Jesus my way again.

Grooooooaaaaaaannnnnnnnn!

90

I want to shout, scream, tell the mole-man to stop staring at me. People continue bobbing their heads up, down, up, down with closed eyes, as if the groaner's constipation is taking them somewhere. The groans make me want to shove the mole-man's head into the toilet. I'm not sure why I agreed to come here. The instructor can sense my resistance, I know it. I can feel it. They don't like me. I'm not fully immersed. Fuck it.

JOHNNY LOCK

After visiting a friend at her new apartment—having gawked from her balcony at the view of the skyscrapers and cranes, the city lights and the northern gridlines pushing back into the horizon—I realised two things:

1.   I needed to move to the city. In an apartment. Here, where everything happened. Where people read books on the lawn of the State Library and where there was always a coffee shop no matter which lane you were in. From her balcony, I could see how far my town was. That was no place for me anymore.

2.   It was time I dropped out of university. Study had become something I used to pass time. A bookmark. A device allowing me to stall the beginning of my career. I had no time to post my poems up, no time to work on my novel, no time to commit to anything other than study, study, study.

It was time I changed my life up.

No more study.

91

A new place.

I could see it now: my own writer's den. The drunken fights at 3 am down below. And me, ever-curious, staring down at them from the height of my own balcony, hoping to be the unseen witness of unfolding chaos in this crazy city of literature.

I headed onto the street, clutching my notebook to my chest, eager to pick up the tales of the city. I felt like a hawk, the way I spotted things everywhere I went, finding poetry in the everyday monotony of the world. My head spun. My whole body ached. Bells rang some way off and police officers directed traffic where the lights had stopped working.

I met a woman named Liz who asked me for change, but instead I gave her my whole pack of cigarettes because why the hell was I smoking? *I don't need this.*

I saw Philipp, the monk made from money, and he tried to convince me to join him in a weekly meditation-and-dinner routine. I thought of suffering and its significance. We all suffered, but some of us just suffered more or less than others. I told myself I had been drowned in the depths of suffering, but then I saw people suffering worse than me.

I crossed the street, pedestrian lights blinking, ticking. A man crossed from the other side, staggering. His mouth twisted and gaped as I passed him. He shouted: 'WELCOME TO MELBOURNE CITY!' I almost wanted to thank him, because I loved this city. *Romanticise the place you live in and it becomes a place you don't feel alienated in.* But he continued. 'MELBOURNE CITY! PAEDOPHILE CITY!'

Reaching the other side of the road, the man yelled like

the world was his audience and he was on a stage, preaching, preaching, preaching about the dangers all around us.

'MELBOURNE CITY! PAEDOPHILE CITY! THEY ALL GET AWAY WITH IT AND WE LOVE THEM FOR IT!'

The city was too much for me. I only stuck up a few of the poems I'd written and then caught my train back to the northern suburbs. Mum was laying on the couch, startled by my return.

'Where have you been?' she asked.

'In the city.'

'By yourself? Be careful. What if someone decides to drive on the footpath and wipe out a bunch of pedestrians?'

I scoffed, taking my jacket off and hanging it on the coat stand, and said, 'If I stay here, I'll be afraid of strangers forever, Ma. I'm done with all that.'

In my room, I hit play on a gentle meditation playlist that put me in the mood to do nothing, be nothing, think nothing. The floor was uncomfortable. I liked this. I thought about where it hurt and drew my attention to those places. My knees. My tailbone. My shoulders. It was a reminder that I was here, that things around me weren't burning down. There were no pitchforks outside my window.

My thoughts wandered and found things to fixate on: that assignment due tomorrow, that phone call I needed to make, the girl I wanted to organise a date with. I breathed in, held, breathed out and repeated and finally I was doing it, I was doing it, my mind was centred on my breaths hitting my upper lip and I was doing it.

I was sitting there without a thought in my mind.

And then it struck me that I was thinking all of this. My mind had been on the whole time. I was doing it all wrong.

JAY KHAN

Day 3
2 pm

My mind starts moving into a weird state. I can hear the cogs of my brain turning, clicking into an abstract rhythm. My eyes flicker, up, down, left, right, beneath my lids. My mouth dries up, crusting at the corners. My body tingles as if a million little maggots are wiggling beneath my skin. THEN! In a flash. I lose complete awareness of my physical body. A new world forms in front of me like dimensional shards melting together. The shards formulate into the sickly-lit hall I'm sitting in. I can feel every sensation inside the room, squeezing me. The breaths of strangers move in and out of their noses, looking like blue smokey snot. SUCK IN. SNORT OUT. SUCK IN. SNORT OUT. Thousands of visible zig-zag particles vibrate around the white light-bars above my body. I'm no longer in my body, I've turned into a strange hovering entity, looking down at myself, sucking, snorting blue smokey snot, in, out, in, out, cross-legged on the floor.

I hover there, staring at myself.
Until the speaker goes,
Grooooooaaaaaaannnnnnnnn!

94

THEN! All goes black. My eyes flicker, the saliva in my mouth starts running, dripping. I open my eyes, wipe my mouth, and find myself back in my real body.

The mole-man coughs into his fist. 'You have permission to continue meditation in your room.'

One by one, strangers rise to their feet, stretch their legs before heading for another round of meditation in their rooms. I can't think of anything worse, so I venture out into the woods on an expedition to hunt for something to write on, so I can take note of the weird experience I just had. Luckily I smuggled a pen in my underpants.

In the forest, I rip bark from the trees with a sharpened stick I secretly made when I was supposed to be meditating. But the bark is too much work, too obvious, eyes are everywhere. They will know what I'm doing when they see the great big bark in my hands. Eyes are watching me. Always. All the time. I can feel them. I hate it here. I go to the toilet and pull my hair. While I'm pulling, I stare at the toilet roll next to me. I tear a piece, put it on my knee and try to write over the thin fabric. It works. Not well. But better than bark. So I steal a roll and put it in my underwear. People give me funny looks when they see a great big bulge around my cock. Luckily nobody is allowed to speak, and thankfully Jesus never saw me dashing to my room.

While everybody meditates, I start writing (what you are reading) three days worth of experiences until, DING! DING! DING! Jesus interrupts me with his gong. It's time to go back.

JOHNNY LOCK

After a night of frantic inspiration, I typed out dozens of poems
on my Remington Quiet-Riter. I revelled in the joy it gave me.
I handed in an assignment late and decided not to hand another
in at all. It was just university. Not failing. My priorities were
realigning: it was passion, art and human connection I cared about
most. Not study, study, study.

I left the house without saying goodbye to Mum, skipping
her usual paranoid lecture about danger entirely. At my local train
station, I posted a poem up on a fibreglass screen and then sat back
and watched commuters stop to read it.

The train ride was a blur and I hardly remembered the
escalators, the Myki machines, the ticket inspectors. I made my
way to the State Library on autopilot. The library looked like
it had become the hub of tragedy, a gloomy locale without its
usual serene beauty. Everyone was dressed in heavy coats and
sunglasses. No one picnicked on the lawn. I wrote about these
observations, paying close attention to a man on the steps—small
frame, tan jacket, face half-covered by a mask too big for his elfish
features.

I scribbled down my observations in my notebook when
I saw a man in all-black storming out of the library. 'Fucking
assholes!' he murmured, descending the steps. 'They do this on
purpose.'

Heads turned to look at him. I flipped to a new page and transcribed what he said: *'They do it deliberately, just to piss me off too, the wankers. It's all me. They all just do this to me. No one else but me.'* I saw the way he registered the avoidance of those around and carried on with his murmuring. Whatever his account may have been of what transpired inside the library, he believed his truth with all of his heart. He wandered down Swanston Street full of bitterness.

Then I spotted a street vendor waving copies of *The Big Issue*. I had no money to buy one this time, but I couldn't help notice the vendor's infectious smile. A positive light in a dark world of pandemics and problems on the street.

I returned to my notebook and wrote a poem.

HOW NOT TO BE BITTER

How not to be bitter
in a world with scarified skeletons
roaming the streets with jolty steps,
dreaming of city snows and
swimming with cynicism,
only to die in an alley
behind a dumpster?

How not to be bitter
in a world where Julie wanders
with her earmuffs
whenever there are sirens
or street cleaners,

clutching the invisible scars
on her wrists?

How not to be bitter
in a world where money-monks
know the root of all suffering
but live in blissful ignorance
of the sufferers overdosing
outside Club X and 7-Eleven
at all hours?

How not to be bitter
in a world where street vendors
selling copies of *The Big Issue*
to the blind foot traffic
still smile and wish
us a 'very good day'
in the face of being ignored?

How not to be bitter
in a world where the bitter ones
claim to possess some truth
that the optimists don't know
and would rather
stamp out optimism
because it's easy?

How not to be bitter
in a world where street-watchers
see all the things you miss
and look at the world
in a way that isn't bitter
to bring the streets
back to life?

JAY KHAN

Day 5
4:30 am

I try to meditate but my throat keeps jamming as if I swallowed
a cactus, GAK! GAK! COUGH! COUGH! The person next to
me clenches his fingers, the person in front of me scratches his
ear, my palms sweat, the person behind me breathes heavily, the
girl with no hair looks at me, two girls huff and puff every time I
cough. They hate me. I can see they hate me, they must hate me,
why are they doing that? Eyes! Eyes are everywhere! Bzzzzz! A
fly lands on my finger. I can feel its minuscule hairs running across
my finger. I need water. GAK! GAK! The mole-man is nowhere
to be seen, just an empty table. My meditation neighbour huffs to
himself. Panting. Aching. Fighting his suffering. He reminds me of
my aching throat. COUGH! COUGH! I shift from one bum cheek
to the other, around the clock. TIK! TOK! TOK! Trying to find
comfort, but nothing is helping. 'One, two, three, four.' I hum to

myself in my mind, hoping to sink into meditation, slowly, calmly, then GAK! GAK! My throat tells me to stop trying. COUGH! COUGH! The room starts spinning. My eyes blur. My fingers, legs, bum cheeks sweat, ache, hurt. Rage seeps into my heart, I can feel it boiling through my toes. I listen to my neighbours suffering and laugh. 'Ha! Ha!' I laugh out loud. 'Ha! Ha!' Strangers open their eyes and stare at me with vicious, anxious intentions. Some curl their lips. Others do nothing but stare. Ha! Ha! Ha! I want to jump up onto my feet, scream in their faces, and throttle their necks. Ha! Ha! Ha! I want to rip my clothes off, swing my penis around and around in circles like a helicopter, spit at the ceiling, eat my fingernails, I want to hit my head through the meditation walls and taste my blood. Hmmmmm. I want to get on all fours like a dog, WOOF! WOOF! I want to pant, sniff, SNIFF! SNIFF! and scurry out of the hall into the forest, barking, sniffing, panting, eating spiders in my path. Gobble, gobble, gobble. Ha! Ha! Ha!

But ...

I don't do any of that.

Instead I sit, silently, with tears in my eyes, trying to piece together my imploded mind. Sadistically giggling to myself. Ha! Ha! Ha! Ha! I look at every stranger in the room, nobody is looking at me. They are too busy melting down in their closed-eye world.

CREAK! A door swings open. The mole-man wanders into the hall, climbs onto his pedestal and asks a row of girls to meditate in front of him. I watch him twiddle his fingers, scratch his nose, fix his underwear. There's something off about this man. I don't know why, but I want to poke his eyes out with my middle finger.

Rage continues to bubble inside of me, deepening, seeping into my joints after every throat curling GAK! GAK! My meditation neighbour, the frail Hispanic man, starts suffering out loud. He whimpers like an injured dog, his breathing gets heavy like a foghorn. I want to smother his face with my cushion. Put him out of his misery. Then he won't have to eat anymore.

Before grabbing my cushion, I jump to my feet, yell 'FUCK' under my breath, run to my dorm before the mole-man can summon me, and curl up in a ball and cry. I cry, sob, wail out loud, scratching the bed, my head, wishing for the ten days to be over. My mind is fragmented, broken. I'm a broken machine with nowhere to go and nothing to do. I want to run away, but I can't. I feel like a raging bull, a wild elephant, a wimp who can't keep silent for ten days. I don't care. Let it be. Let me cry. I don't care!!!! I do as I like! HA! HA! GAHHHHHHHH! GAK! GAK! COUGH! COUGH!

JOHNNY LOCK

One day after a night shift at the bookshop, I headed to a bus stop to wait for my ride home. There were a few others on the seats, including a lanky dark-skinned man that turned to me as I flipped a page of the book I was reading.

'Have you ever wanted to leave earth?' he asked.

I glanced up from my book. It didn't look like I would finish the chapter by the time the bus arrived. 'I guess so.'

'Ever wanted to go to some other planet?'

'It would be nice.'

'Me,' he said, hand on chest. 'I'd happily take up the opportunity to go to another planet, if it meant I could never return to earth. That's something I've always dreamed of. If you achieve your dreams, why go back to what came before? It's rising above, you know? It's transcendence. Once you reach it, you can't go any higher. So why bother going back down? You'll only be dreaming to go back up again.'

He told me we would be stupid to fear going above—that it's the most blissful thing we could hope for.

'Hope,' he said, staring at the wall of the bus shelter, then at the seat, then into the depths of my eyes like he knew he was reaching right inside me, speaking to the dreamer in me, the escapist who had lived there all those years. 'Hope that you experience nirvana when you take off, when you reach the height of your ascendance. You heard of nirvana? It's a Buddhism thing. Enlightenment. Don't fear that the height won't be bliss, that you won't be able to return. The height will be bliss—that's all it can be. And the return doesn't matter, only the rising matters!'

Everyone else at the bus stop ignored him, staring straight ahead as if he wasn't here, or looking down at their phones and putting their headphones in so they didn't have to hear.

But I heard him.

Was he an imaginary friend? Was I the only one at the bus stop who accepted his experience and was willing to let him speak about it? Maybe that was because I learned to listen to people's stories—to really listen—from Jay. He might have been a storyteller, but he was an even better listener when the time called for it. Now I was the listener, the only person who could see the lanky man, hear the lanky man, feel the passion in the lanky man's acid rambling. I had felt the desire to transcend too. Why shouldn't I have listened? Didn't everyone want to transcend, sooner or later? I knew what he was talking about, or thought I knew.

I told him he made perfect sense and that he probably had more knowledge about this than any of us at the bus stop. When my bus arrived and I boarded, the lanky man still smiled at me through the window.

JAY KHAN

Day 7

Days have moved on since my throat cleared. The mole-man has taken us further into meditation. He presses a button. 'I want you to meditate for one hour without moving a muscle,' explains the groaning man from the speakers. 'Use your determination to make it through the hour.' I think back to the past six days. I hadn't lasted longer than ten minutes in one position. The recording ends. I hear the birds yapping in the trees, the wind rustling through the bushes. I settle into a comfy position and start the challenge.

5 minutes pass. I want to move.

10 minutes pass. I want to scratch my nose.

15 minutes pass. I feel as if somebody has taken a sledge hammer to my ankles.

30 minutes pass. Pain has taken hold of every nerve in my body. My eyes tear up. My mouth drools. My ear itches.

Everything feels fuzzy and painful. 40 minutes pass.

I want to scream. My neighbour howls, whimpers, cries, annoying everybody in the room but himself.

THEN! In a surreal moment, everything makes sense. His howls make me happy. I realise how he's doing it all wrong. He's continuously fighting the pain, constantly running away from discomfort. And when I think this way, my pain shifts into a strange unified feeling, a sort of revelation throughout my body. A million euphoric maggots wriggle through my body. An appreciation comes to mind for discomfort, struggle, pain. I think about a man I saw in Melbourne, struggling, panting, wheeling himself up a hill in a wheelchair. He made me think about my legs, and how much of a privilege it is to feel something, anything, even pain. I'm sure he would give up anything to feel something one more time, even a sledge hammer to his legs.

Grooooooaaaaaaaannnnnnnn! the groaning man trapped inside the speaker groans.

One hour has passed since I've not moved. My neighbour looks to be on the brink of collapse, his bald patch looks bigger. The mole-man tells us to go back to our rooms to meditate alone. I smile, looking at the marks on my hands, the same marks the psychic told me run short.

RICK WALKOW

Absence was a weird, weird thing. After moments of brief
excitement, we eventually had to return to the mundane all over
again. A few days after parting from Johnny and Jay, I walked
around the city's streets with the lingering scent of the adventures
we had. I looked at St Paul's Cathedral and thought about Johnny
and his string of rambles, Jay and his boldness as he trailed off into
the streets. But the two of them faded in and out of my memory
like lingering ghosts.

Days after the first shots of adventure with them, I decided
to move into the city to integrate myself into the action and bustle.
When I was younger, I always loved taking the train into the busy
streets and basking in the sounds of the passing trams, the buskers
who nodded whenever they heard the clinks of coins in their guitar
cases, and the groans of yuppies on their way to work. Now after
years of back and forth, I was tired of the train rides interrupting
the flow of the city. So I booked an apartment inspection with the
intention of landing a place. It was my attempt to bring the city to
my backyard, so the rhythm was accessible the minute I exited my
front door.

It was a Friday morning and Melbourne was on the verge
of autumn. I circled around the block and ended up on Lonsdale
Street. It was such a busy district that cars constantly honked at
one another, but compared to the constant construction work, I had
nothing to complain about. I went to the address of the apartment

building and spotted a lobby that was bearable. It was pretending to be something it wasn't with its marbled floor and landing mirrors, but it was something I could live with. I stood below in the streets and spotted a young woman in a brown overcoat. She looked around the block, looked up at the building, and I walked up to her.

'Are you also here for the inspection?'

She turned to me. A second later, she said, 'Sure,' and gave me one of those 'nice to meet you' smiles. I looked into the streets and saw a balding short man in a suit coming toward us in rapid steps. Everything about him slipped into the perfect description of a real estate agent. They were people I would never become, but nevertheless still needed.

The girl said, 'So, why an apartment in the city centre?' She took a step back and tried to figure me out. 'What do you do?'

'I'm a writer,' I said and immediately regretted it. 'I mean, I'm also a student. Are you studying too?'

'I'm studying a master's,' she said. She turned to the approaching real estate agent. I waved at him. 'Do you know him?'

'Him? No,' I gave a dry laugh. I didn't have to know a real estate agent to wave at him.

He was short and had a bit of a Russian accent. 'Hey. I'm Mark.' He reached out his hand and his shake was firm. 'Shall we?'

He buzzed open the front door to the lobby and led us in. The first apartment suite we inspected looked like a college dorm and I shook my head. It was nothing like the pictures. Even the most experienced interior designer couldn't turn that place around. The girl had the same disgusted look about her.

We both exited the room and Mark greeted us with a smile.

'How was everything?'

The girl and I looked at each other and Mark got the drift. 'Well, there's another unit upstairs ...'

We ducked into a lift. A few floors up, we ended up in another suite. Mark opened the door and I liked the place immediately. The space was quaint and bare, but I thought with a little work, it could turn into a dream suite.

I turned to the girl and she nodded. 'Needs some cleaning.'

'Lots of cleaning.' I looked out of the window and saw an old church across the street. 'This is the place I think.'

She turned to me like I was a mad person. 'Are you sure?'

'Yeah.' My warm breath fogged the cold glass. 'I really like it.'

'See ... I don't know.' She lingered for a moment before turning her gaze toward the doorway.

Mark greeted us at the elevator with a binder full of paperwork. 'So,' he said, 'if you're interested, when do you guys want to move in?'

'Huh?' We looked at each other.

Mark waited for a response.

The girl took a step away from me with widened eyes.

'We're not a couple,' I said.

'Oh! I'm so sorry.' Mark scratched the patch where his hair used to be. 'Follow me then.'

We went into the elevator. On our way down to the ground floor, Mark kept giving me side glances. Right before the elevator dinged at the sight of G on the display, he shoved a piece of paper in my hand. 'Alright, if you pay the bond and the first month of rent, you could move in by Thursday.' He said in that urgent, inflated voice, reminding me of an auctioneer. He turned to the girl and shoved another piece in her hand. She held the page and looked at me with raised eyebrows.

We exited the elevator and I shook Mark's hand. 'I'm taking it,' I said.

'Yes ... yes. Good,' he said. 'Just get the paperwork through and we ...' Real Estate agents were a restless bunch. 'Sorry, I've got another in ... five minutes. So, just email ... Nice to meet you ... Later!'

I stood in the early autumn wind with the girl and we looked at one another.

'Remember,' she said with a smile. 'Needs some cleaning.'

I examined the paperwork and nodded. 'Lots of cleaning.'

JAY KHAN

Day 8

The final days are upon us. Everybody is in the meditation hall apart from me. I skipped class since I know the mole-man will be in his house sleeping. He only comes out for the mandatory meditation sessions. There's only so long you can spend in your mind before it tells you to get out. I tried sleeping through the meditation sessions yesterday but as soon as I fell asleep the mole-man sent Jesus to wake me up ... 'You're distracting the others,' he said.

There's a giant tree outside the meditation hall. It's pale, yellow and old. During my last meditation session, I think of a game. 'How many times can I walk backwards around the big tree without vomiting?'

I start walking. One, two, twenty-six, forty-five, eighty-one, eighty-two, eighty-three …

'Jay, stop it.' hisses Jesus from the front of the mediation hall, rushing out, oohing and ahhing over his naked feet on sharp twigs. 'You're distracting the others.'

I carry on spinning. I don't care! He rushes over, grabs my wrist, and tells me, 'You're ruining people's experience. Stop it!' I say nothing and head into the woods to play with my secret spear.

RICK WALKOW

With a stupid smile on my face, I wandered the streets, envisioning what life would be like to live in the heart of the city. At the General Post Office, I stopped. A tram clanged on my left and I saw a poem on the wall. It looked like someone had just pasted it not long ago. 'Johnny,' I chuckled. I read it and realised he was probably also going around the streets of the city, craving the same lingering scent of adventure as me.

I sat down on the steps of the General Post Office and enjoyed the clanging trams, the coin clatters in the guitar cases, and the occasional sighs and moans from the yuppies. Only this time, I knew all of this—plus more—was in my reach, without the lingering fear of having to catch a train back to my old suburban home.

JAY KHAN

Day 10

DING! DING! Our time is up. We have reached the end of the road to enlightenment. Jesus hovers from disciple to disciple shaking hands. Mole-man disappears into his cabin one last time. The lady with cotton-white hair congratulates us for our mental stamina and tells us we are now followers of Dharma. My table-neighbour's fingers rattle against the table, shaking, shaking.

Ten people on a bus. Travelling out of a forest. To civilisation.

The firefighter with soft short blonde hair and a strong face looked at me. 'How are you feeling?'

I looked at him, juddering from side to side, crammed inside a bus, riding down, down, down out of some Tasmanian forest into civilisation with a phone. 'I feel alright.'

Echo looked out of the window, at all the passing trees, looking confused. Frank said nothing. The bus juddered.
The skinny Hispanic man twitched at the eyes. The Chinese businessman shouted, 'I've done five of these now.'

I said nothing.

One was enough for me.

There's a tale to this city

DAY 7

08:00 - 09:00

I started meditation with phlegm in my throat. That didn't want to go away. I tried and tried to forget, but still it hung onto my throat in great thick globs, trying to get my attention to react. I started feeling rage enter my mind, doubt I can get past it. I battled with it and battled it, failing every time. Always making me gulp. But still i did not move my legs, arms, and hands, for the hour. Then, something told me, "If you won't accept the phlegm is there, because it is, that is the reality,

Then how can you expect to accept the painful memories of the past. Because just like the you try to run away, or each time

112

...ke up at 4 with a excruciating
sore throat. I didnt drink much water
yesterday. I go to ...rhate in hall
but throat stops my breathing. I
... after 5 mins and go to sleep
Im not supposed to, I'm supposed to be
meditating but fuck it! HA!
I wone up at 6:30 for breakfast.
I feel so good. Not drained and
brain dead. People have to be strugg-
ing today. My table neigbour h...
h oon raging all day yesterday and
today I w... find the struggle. I
come to the realisation, dont want
to be a saint or a Buddah I just
...... to be me (...) neither
... ... cam this. I'm becoming
more and rebellious by the day
A... ...ing it. Not the course,
I hate it here. But the feeling
of rebellion. I rarely rebel. And
...y the power of ...ny anybody.
over. I refuse to treat the teacher
as a god. He's just a man like
myself ...

IT'S ABOUT TIME

JOHNNY LOCK

When Jay returned from Tasmania, the three of us reconvened in an upstairs bar. He told us his wild stories of meditation-gone-wrong. It felt as if he'd never left. But then he dropped the nuclear bomb and I had to order another drink to process it:

'I'm leaving in three months,' he said. 'My visa's expiring.'

We wandered the streets and wrote stories in our notebooks, but I felt myself slipping into an unnatural pattern of rambling thoughts. Impermanence. Time. Change. I tried to shudder the thoughts away, but I carried them with me through the city.

Jay made us meditate on the steps of the General Post Office. I crossed my legs and waited for his instruction.

'Don't you think it's a little noisy?' Rick asked. A woman and her two children stopped at the Public Purse, a clam-like granite seat outside the GPO. One of her children climbed on the structure like a mountain climber. The other clung to his mother's leg and wailed.

I twiddled my thumbs. 'I've never meditated in public before. I don't know how I'm going to go with all these distractions and that crying fucking child.'

Jay shut his eyes, shut the world out, shut us out. 'Just close your eyes. Ten minutes. If your mind wanders, bring it back to your breathing.' I closed my eyes, but peeped them open to see if Rick was doing the same. He wasn't. His eyes swung between the passersby and the trams and the pigeons. He noticed me looking at him and surrendered. I closed my eyes again.

My breath on my upper lip.

My breath on my upper lip.

There's another tram.

Are those sirens? Police? Ambos?

That child is still crying.

I heard that child's screechy wail every day for the next three months. We wrote down our stories and they became a scattered mess. Jay suggested we put them together into one volume to make sense of them all. Rick and I grinned. We compiled the stories. And then Jay's time was up.

JAY KHAN

TIK! TOK! TIK! TOK! the clock went, ever since landing back in Melbourne.

Time passed unorderly, as if I fell into some sort of foggy hole and crawled out three months later. Days, weeks, months passed like one long day broken up by various stories I collected inside the fog.

Since landing back in the city, much had happened.

Rick moved to the city, Johnny dropped out of university, and I unexpectedly received a sponsorship to become a full-time writer.

The three of us hovered through the streets, listening to the souls living between the cracks of the city. Behind all the cafes, restaurants, dumpsters, and universities. Writing their words into our jumbled notebooks.

RICK WALKOW

As people get older, it gets easier and easier to say goodbye. All it takes is a step onto a train, a smile with a turned head or a final hug before walking off.

'I ain't giving you a hug.' I shook my head as Jay paced around Flinders Street station.

'But I'm leaving.' He had his bag with him and his plane was about to leave in three hours.

` 'Didn't your ass just land back here three months ago?' I said

'This is it.' He shrugged. 'I've got time for one more coffee.'

'Where's Johnny?' I looked around. The station felt dated and boring, the same way my new apartment had lost its charm after a few months. The city was my backyard, but it had already turned into a new mundane.

'He said he's ...' Jay glanced at the entrance of the station. Johnny walked into view, wearing his winter jacket. He gave me a whack on the back.

'What took you so long?' I asked.

'Ah, well ...' Before Johnny could fire up a ramble, Jay said, 'This is it, isn't it? One more coffee.' He smiled, bringing me back to that hot summer's day when I first met him. The flip-flops, the t-shirt with three naked ladies, and that stupid haircut. At the time, he was just another stranger I'd met with my usual regard and suspicion. But time had transfigured him into someone I knew; a someone in a puffer jacket, with a bag full of notebooks he'd gathered in Melbourne, and a slightly better haircut.

'Let's head to that French place again, shall we?' I said before crossing the street. Johnny and Jay lingered behind before they caught up. We eventually ended up in the cafe alleyway and sat down at our regular table. A waiter came over and I looked up. *'Trois personnes, merci.'*

JAY KHAN

'I'll have what he's having,' I said to the waiter, referring to Johnny's latte. Rick smirked to himself and started jibba-jabbering in French to the waiter.

While Rick rambled, and Johnny sat there patiently, a strange hand touched my back. I looked over to find a black-and-white lion with red eyes staring at me from the surface of the hand.

Johnny and Rick stared at the stranger's 'you got any change?' fingers with empty eyes.

'Look who it is!' I said, pulling my mask under my chin, staring at a white bushy beard with two eyes.

'It's you!' the stranger shrieked, tugging at his fraying blue mask. 'How did my story come out?'

'Not bad, Michael the Archangel, not bad. I will get the boys to give you the story next week. My time's fallen short, pal. I'm leaving the city today.'

Michael tugged at his orange nicotine-stained moustache. 'Is that right?'

Silence fell between us.

'It's about time I leave now. I've been here long enough. My visa's running out. No point overstaying my welcome. Gotta keep moving, you know how it is.'

'Hmmmm, you've got to go frame those letters of yours before you leave then, so those dickhead street sweepers don't throw them away like the others. If you're gone, who's going to tell our stories?'

Johnny waved his hand, smiling sheepishly. 'I can.'

'Who is he?' Michael asked impatiently.

'My friend. He's a poet. A pretty good one. He can take over as the storyteller of the street.'

'Hmmmm …' He scratched his moustache. 'I need to shave this thing, some fella told me I look like a tangerine this morning. Said I need to stop smoking. Does it look bad, Jay?'

'Not at all, Michael. It's unique. I would keep it if I were you. Your orange moustache and your red-eyed lion give you character. Look at these,' I said, showcasing my bottom row of teeth, jagged and wonky in every way. 'They're as crooked as a politician, but shit, I like them that way, they make me feel like a shark, BITE! BITE! Ha! Ha!'

'Hmmm … you might be right there, you crazy fool.'

Rick pulled out his wallet and asked, 'Have you had breakfast, Michael?'

'Huh!' he yelled.

'Here, take this.' Rick passed him a five-dollar note. 'Get yourself some food.'

'Thank you, fella. Jay, your friends are a good pair of cunts, aren't they?'

'Yes, Michael, they are.'

'Alright, well, I'll be off then, you know how it is. Somebody's gotta work, 'ent they?'

'Sure do mate. Take it easy, yeah?'

'Take it easy. See you on the other side, my friend.'

Before trailing off into the distance, he shouted, 'Remember what I said, "Time. Time. Time. Where did time go?"'

I continued the sentences he had told me weeks before. '"Are we here, there, or everywhere? There is another world. Where it is, we don't know."'

The waiter returned. Asked if we wanted food. We said no. He asked again. Eventually he surrendered and left us with our coffee.

Rick said, 'Sometimes, when we write about people, I feel bad not giving them anything in return.'

Johnny looked over at his coffee, stirring his cup, saying nothing.

'I don't feel bad,' I said, 'we are sharing their stories. Money isn't the only way to give back.'

'Sure ... but, don't you feel like we're using them?'

'Not really. Do you feel like you're using me?'

'I don't catch your drift.'

'I mean ... when I tell you stories and you write them down, do you feel like you're using me?'

'I don't know.'

'I don't think you're using me, Rick. I'm happy you wrote something I said. Most folk like to be heard. They like to feel as if their words hold some sort of value. When you're dead, you're dead. And no cosmetic thing can keep you alive. But our words, our stories, our wisdom ... these are the only things that can keep us alive, in spirit. If it's not written down, our entire existence will fade away faster than that birdshit next to your foot.'

JOHNNY LOCK

I watched Jay's frame bounce down the street, and only then did I realise the profound impact he'd had on my life. He passed out of sight, lost in the crowd of strangers, and I was flooded with memories of the first time we met. The steps of Flinders. The exorcism. The first strangers he'd introduced me to. I'd been so paranoid then. A whole other person. Fidgety, rambly and full of excuses.

Rick clinked his cup of coffee against mine. 'Time has gone by so fast, don't you think?'

'It's flown by,' I said. I zoned out, my eyes fixed on a man in bulky headphones shuffling along behind Rick. The man reminded me of Julie, the paranoid woman in pink, with her big earmuffs and her stories about police and handcuffs. And to think that day was at the beginning of the year. It felt like it had happened in another time, in a city I was still a stranger to, even though I'd been calling it 'home'.

I cleared my throat. 'I sometimes ... still think it's January. Do you know what I mean?'

'I have no idea what you mean.'

'Well … that was when we met, the three of us. January. Crazy, right?'

'Nuts,' Rick agreed. He bobbed his head to the flow of French tunes, trailing out from the doors of the new cafe—an upgrade from its previous locale in the same alleyway. The French cafe had been smaller and a little cramped, but the upgrade had a large indoor dining area and a few round tables-and-chairs outside as placeholders, where the original cafe had been. Rick sighed and downed the rest of his coffee. 'Ah, how things change.'

'Change.' I let the scary word hang between us. 'A terrifying and exciting concept. I bet the philosophers have a lot to say about change.'

Rick smirked. 'Oh, they do. Speaking of change … what's next for you? You've made some pretty big changes recently.'

'Oh … you know.' I shrugged. 'Moving time.'

'Are you bringing all your books with you to your new apartment?'

'All seven-hundred.'

'You're insane.'

'You think I could part with them? Not a chance in the world. My new apartment better have a balcony. I can't wait to watch the drunks struggling to make their way home in the early hours of the morning. I'll sip my coffee up there, smoke a cigarette or three and enjoy my new writer's den.'

Rick nudged me. 'It's all coming together. This is it.'

I realised that this *was* it. I'd dreamed about changing my life up for so long that I was living in a fantasy I was yet to create:

the ideal life of a poet here in the big city, away from the troubles of suburbia. But I'd hardly registered the fact that I was at the threshold of actualising these changes. I dropped out of university to pursue my career as a writer. *That should get me into some trouble.* I applied for a new bookstore job not far from where I used to study. *Hopefully then I'll have the money to get the hell out of this depressing town.* And I fell head over heels for a girl. *The old me didn't think I was worth loving.*

The old me lived in a state of permanent distress. Crumbling at the idea of deadlines and university assignments. My desk was piled with books, papers, sticky notes, clothes yet to be folded or hung up, a broken hourglass, scattered piles of old polaroids. My new life wasn't even a reflection of the old me. Time. Change. Things that used to terrify me. But I was beginning to like the gifts that they brought. Time and change brought Jay and Rick to me. I wondered who I'd be today had I never stepped out my door, had I heeded my mother's warnings about meeting strangers. Most likely, I'd still be cautiously avoiding the outdoors, hiding away with my books and falling prey to all that paranoia nonsense.

I finished the dregs of my latte. 'Hey Rick …' I said. 'What did Jay mean when he told Michael the Archangel that I'm going to tell the stories now?'

'I think he means you'll be the eyes on the street in his place,' Rick said. 'The street needs a writer's pair of eyes to pick up all the idiosyncrasies. All that madness out there. And you won't be alone. I'm still here.'

'You're right.'

A clocktower bell struck at the hour. The waiter collected our empty cups and I was already craving another.

'I can't help but feel bummed out that Jay's gone, though,' I murmured. 'Will we ever see him again?'

Rick wiped the fog from his glasses. 'I have no doubt that bastard will show up in our lives again. He's not finished with us. You *will* continue with your street poems, right?'

'Oh, man. I've only just started with the street poems. I've already got one stewing in my brain right now, sitting here with you.'

Time and Change

Time is coffee at the French cafe
with old buddies parting ways.

   It's meditating down south
and writing on toilet paper,
because the monks refuse
to let you write or speak;

   It's looking for a new home
and being screwed around
by plumbers who see no need
to make time for you;

   It's roaming the alleys
and sticking your words

on the many brick walls
of the city you dream of;

  It's when visas expire
and planes take off
and the world is different,
because of three pairs of eyes
roaming the streets.

Time is ticking, ticking,
and burning just enough
to keep the embers hot.

Change is not getting to see
your old buddies for drinks anymore.

  It's the death of paranoia
and the birth of confidence,
everything new, everything fresh
and full of poetic wonder;

  It's the act of giving up
and trying something else,
your old plans scrapped
for new and improved ones;

  It's being drunk on new things
and accepting the crash,

a chance at trying again,
and not wallowing in failure.

Change is happening now,
so we may as well embrace it, right?
We'd be stupid not to.

What change the future brings
is breathtaking and bewildering;
there's nothing frightening there,
not when it brings so much potential —
and I am ready.

RICK WALKOW

Johnny walked off from the cafe with a bag full of poems. 'In a bit,
I've got to walk around.'

'Later.' I nodded, placed a tip on the table, and went back
to my building. Melbourne was heading into winter. I braced the
wind and returned to an empty apartment. After months of getting
the place in order, it finally felt a little bit like home. I went into the
kitchen and poured myself a glass of water.

'*You motherfucker.*'

Jay's voice came from the living room, from a passing
memory. I scanned around the living room. I brewed some tea, sat
on the couch.

'I feel like for years I've just been chasing goal after goal after goal ...'

I sipped my tea.

'... haven't learned how to live yet.'

'You know,' Jay said, *'for me it's the opposite. I've spent so much time living and not enough time just ... settling and chasing goals. For so long I thought I was living in a dream but now I just feel like ... that was so empty.'*

He reminded me of some long-lost brother who was a little fucked up when he ran away from home. Like brotherly love, there were unspoken words and silent nods that brought us close. But also like brotherly love, I would always miss him when he was off on the road all over again. Melbourne was my home, but Jay had other plans.

'Let's meet in Paris after I leave.' His voice lingered in the room.

'Sure thing,' I replied to empty space. All new adventures start with some elusive promise, some distant adventure. *'Jay, I wished that you'd never leave.'*

'It's complicated, man,' he said. *'But I'll try. You bet your balls, I'll try.'* He settled down his cup. *'I gotta bounce, man. See you later.'* I waved him goodbye and he ran into the corridor.

I smiled and reached for my mug. There was only one resting on the coffee table. There was no trace of him in my apartment.

I took my bag and went to the library to get some air.

After finding a seat, I saw a woman on the verge of crashing asleep at the table across from me, her bags scattered next to her. I wondered what she had been through and if this was what it was like to hit the road, hit the streets in that fervour only possessed by younglings. She didn't look young, which was probably why she was so tired and on the verge of a nap. And then and there, I thought about Jay constantly dashing about, trying to bring a fervour to the cold streets. My entire life was flipped upside down because of him.

I exited the library, my eyes fixed on the church across the street I had passed a thousand times before. The day was old but the night was young, and Jay was out there on the streets somewhere,

dashing,
dashing,
dashing ...

TO BE CONTINUED

'Everyday at five, I would talk to John on the corner of Bourke Street. An old man with thick hands and a bushy beard, sitting on a green milk crate cushioned by cardboard.'

'Then and there, an ambulance stopped on the other side of the street, in front of an adult video store.'

'Don't you think it's a little noisy?' Rick asked. A woman and her two children stopped at the Public Purse, a clam-like granite seat outside the GPO.'

'People who write together usually start from a humble place. Sometimes it was the backlot of a theatre or after a university class. For the three of us, it was at a little cafe where French tunes echoed against two buildings.'

'He dragged me into a side alley. The brick walls on either side were covered in street art, picture frames, and broken glass.'

'Where the hell are you taking me?'
He smirked. 'The Land of Sunshine. I thought you knew this city.'

'Flinders Street station, at 10 am.'

'I saw a man sitting alone, where you're sitting right now. He was writing with a
fountain pen made of solid gold ...'

'When he rambled and rambled and rambled, his eyes shone like jades in the sky, green on the verge of blue ...'

'I'm already mad,' Jay laughed. 'Now shut up. Let's get some stories.'

'I wanted to prop a skull on my desk in the middle of the night, so I could stare into its empty eye sockets and shout: *what the hell are you looking at?*'

ABOUT THE AUTHORS

R. C. Waldun is a writer, speaker, and social critic based in
Melbourne, Australia whose work mainly consists of criticisms
of the modern education system and ways toward a better literary
education. For more creative projects, head to rcwaldun.com

Jay is a writer from a village in the middle of nowhere who moves
around posting letters on walls. You can find his work on Instagram
and YouTube @jaytheauthor

Jaidyn L Attard is a writer, poet and editor from Naarm
(Melbourne) who sticks his typewritten poetry up on the walls
of the city. He currently works in a bookstore and is a hoarder of
books because of this. You can view his poems on instagram @
jaidynpoetry

There's a tale to this city

THERE'S A TALE TO THIS CITY

Jay, the restless wanderer, rocks the lives of two strangers by introducing them to the strange world he has stumbled across—the streets of Melbourne. Rick, the bookworm, is torn away from his mundane academic life. Johnny, the paranoid poet, is released from his small-town worries.

When they hit the streets together, twisted tales rise from the gutters. *The bathing man. The cardboard preacher. The mute who isn't a mute.* The trio cast aside everything they know, embarking on a journey to meet the city's neglected souls.

There's a Tale to This City is an offbeat portrait of Melbourne that combines poetry, narrative prose and toilet paper diary entries, recollecting the strange experiences of three writers, who came together to learn the art of listening.

Lightning Source UK Ltd.
Milton Keynes UK
UKHW012333071121
393571UK00001B/2